THE
NUTCRACKER

THE
NUTCRACKER

ALEXANDRE DUMAS

FALL RIVER PRESS

New York

FALL RIVER PRESS

New York

An Imprint of Sterling Publishing Co., Inc.

Cover illustration © 2018 Sterling Publishing Co., Inc.
Introduction © 2018 Sterling Publishing Co., Inc.

This story was first published in English in 1847 under
the title *The History of a Nutcracker*.

This 2018 edition printed for Barnes & Noble Booksellers, Inc.
by Sterling Publishing Co., Inc.

ISBN 978-1-4351-5452-0

Manufactured in India

2 4 6 8 10 9 7 5 3

sterlingpublishing.com

Cover design by Danielle Deschenes
Endpapers courtesy Dover Publications

CONTENTS

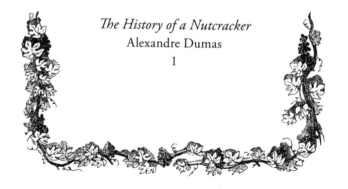

INTRODUCTION

Every Christmas, millions of people young and old delight in *The Nutcracker* ballet, which tells the story of an enchanted nutcracker who one Christmas night is turned into a handsome prince through the love of a young girl, and who takes her on a fantastic journey to a magical land of sweets and spices. The ballet's score, by renowned Russian composer Pyotr Ilyich Tchaikovsky, has become a beloved Christmas tradition, as recognizable as any Christmas carol or holiday song. Yet for all the popularity of this holiday confection, few people are aware that the ballet has its origins in a work of fiction written almost three-quarters of a century before its first staging, one that is very different in its telling from the story most see unfold on the ballet stage, or play on television and movie screens.

The story behind *The Nutcracker* is the creation of Ernst Theodor Amadeus Hoffmann (1776–1822), a Prussian civil servant who wrote fiction in his free time between postings that took him from Warsaw to Berlin. In his novels and stories Hoffmann, a progressive thinker, celebrated the power of art and the imagination to excite the mind and awaken the spirit. The tale of fantasy proved the perfect vehicle for what Hoffmann hoped to achieve through his writing, and his first collection of fantasies, published in 1814, earned him an appreciative audience among adult readers. Hoping similarly to reach younger readers, in 1816 Hoffman contributed two stories to a two-volume anthology of fairy tales. Among them was the tale whose title translates as "The Nutcracker and the Mouse King," which he had written for the children of his colleague and fellow civil servant Julius Hitzig.

Hoffmann later included "The Nutcracker and the Mouse King" in his four-volume compilation *The Serapion Brethren* (1819–1822). The fictional Serapions are a quartet of storytellers modeled on the literary salon that Hoffman himself presided over in Berlin, and their discussions about the interplay between the real and the imagined in the text that frames each story very probably echo those of their real-life counterparts. Lothair, the teller of "The Nutcracker and the Mouse King," defends it against his colleagues' criticisms that it will baffle younger readers, saying, "I think it is a great mistake to suppose that clever, imaginative children—and it is only they who are in question here—should content themselves with the empty nonsense which is so often set before them under the name Children's Tales. They want something much better; and it is surprising how much they see and appreciate which escapes a good, honest, well-informed papa." By including it in a book that also features tales for adults, Hoffmann clearly indicated that he did not think the story would be of interest only to children.

Credit for the widespread popularity that the story of the Nutcracker has achieved since is due largely to French author Alexandre Dumas (1802–1870), who in 1845 adapted a version of Hoffmann's tale as an entertainment for younger readers under the title *The History of a Nutcracker*. One of the bestselling writers of the nineteenth century, Dumas rendered his version of Hoffmann's tale during the same years that saw the publication of his immensely popular novels *The Three Musketeers* and *The Count of Monte Cristo*. It was translated from the French into English in 1847 as part of London book publisher Chapman and Hall's Picture Story Books series for young readers, featuring more than two hundred illustrations by Georges Bertall (reproduced throughout this edition), who had also illustrated an edition of the fairy tales of Hans Christian Andersen. It was Dumas's more precious treatment of Hoffmann's complex fairy tale that caught the eye of Ivan Vsevolozhsky, director of Russia's Imperial Theatres, in the early 1890s. Vsevolozhsky recommended the tale to Imperial Ballet Master Marius Petipa for adaptation to the ballet stage by Tchaikovsky, and Petipa wrote the libretto to pair with Tchaikovsky's score. *The Nutcracker* debuted at the St. Petersburg Imperial Theatre in 1892. It was only a modestly popular ballet until 1954, when New York City Ballet choreographer George Balanchine presented the version that has become the standard for more than half a century.

As with Hoffman's tale, Dumas's *The History of a Nutcracker* presents a much fuller story than that distilled into the ballet libretto, one that includes the years-long history of the nutcracker's origins and enchantment, and an account of how it came into the possession of the enigmatic Herr Drosselmayer. Though it presents a different, and sometimes darker, Nutcracker than the elegant showpiece that has come down to us from ballet stage and screen, it still glimmers with the magic that has made the story, like the ballet, a classic Christmas fantasy and a timeless tale of wonder.

[*The publishers would like to thank Douglas A. Anderson and the Cotsen Children's Library of Princeton University for their invaluable assistance in the preparation of this book.*]

The Nutcracker.

THE NUTCRACKER

※

PREFACE

Which Shows How the Author was Forced to Relate the History of the Nutcracker of Nuremberg

There was a juvenile party at the house of my friend Lord M——; and I had helped to add to the number and noise of the company by taking my little daughter.

It is true that in half an hour, during which I joined in four or five games of blind-man's buff, hot cockles, and hunt the slipper—in spite of the noise which was made by a couple of dozen delightful little rogues from eight to ten years old, and who seemed to try which would talk the loudest—I slipt out of the drawing-room, and sought a certain snug parlour which I knew, and where I hoped to enjoy a little peace for an hour or so.

I had effected my retreat with as much skill as success, escaping not only without being perceived by the juvenile guests, which was not very difficult, considering how intent they were upon their games, but also unnoticed by their parents, which was not so easy a matter. I had reached the wished-for parlour, when I observed, on entering it, that it was for the moment converted into a supper-room, the side boards being heaped up with confectionary and other refreshments. Now as these appearances seemed to promise that I should not be disturbed until supper-time, I threw myself into a comfortable arm-chair, quite delighted with the idea that I was about to enjoy an hour's peace after the dreadful noise which had deafened me in the drawing-room.

I don't know exactly how it was, but at the end of about ten minutes I fell fast asleep.

I cannot say how long I had thus lost all knowledge of what was passing around, when I was suddenly aroused by loud peals of laughter. I opened my eyes in terror, and saw nothing but the beautifully-painted ceiling over my head. Then I tried to get up; but the attempt was useless, for I was fastened to my chair as firmly as Gulliver was on the shore of Lilliput.

I immediately understood in what a scrape I had got myself: I had been surprised in the enemy's country, and was a prisoner of war.

The best thing for me to do in such a case was to put a good face upon the matter, and entreat for my liberty.

My first proposal was to take my conquerors the very next morning to Farrance's, and treat them to anything they liked; but, unhappily, the moment was not well chosen for such an offer: I was addressing myself to an audience already well stuffed with tarts, and whose hands were filled with patties.

My proposal was therefore refused in plain terms.

I then offered to take the entire party to Vauxhall next evening, and amuse them with the exhibition of fire-works.

The proposal was well-received by the little boys; but the little girls would not listen to it, because they were dreadfully afraid of fire-works: they could not endure the noise of the crackers, and the smell of the gunpowder annoyed them.

I was about to make a third offer, when I heard a sweet little musical voice whispering in the ears of a companion certain words which made me tremble: "Ask papa, who writes novels, to tell us some pretty story."

I was on the point of protesting against this; but my voice was drowned by cries of "Oh! yes, a story—we will have a story!"

"But, my dear children," I said, as loud as I could, "you ask me the most difficult thing in the world. A story indeed! Ask me to recite one of Gay's fables, or *My Name is Norval*, if you will; and I may consent. But a story!"

"We don't want anything out of the *Speaker*," cried the children altogether: "we want a story!"

"My dear little friends, if—"

"There is no *if* in the cause: we will have a story!"

"But, my dear little friends, I say again—"

"There is no *but*: we will have a story!"

"Yes: we will have a story! we will have a story!" now echoed on all sides, and in a manner which was too positive to object to any longer.

"Well," I said with a sigh: "if you must, you must."

"Ah! that's capital," cried my little tormentors.

"But I must tell you one thing," said I: "the story I am about to relate is not my own."

"Never mind that, so long as it amuses us."

I must confess that I was a little vexed to think that my audience set so light a value upon my own writings.

"Whose tale is it, then, sir!" asked a pretty voice, belonging, no doubt, to some little being more curious than the others.

"It is by Hoffmann, miss. Have you ever heard of Hoffmann?"

"No, sir; I never heard of him."

"And what is the name of your story, sir?" asked a young gentleman, who, being the son of the nobleman that gave the party, felt a right to question me.

"*The History of a Nutcracker*," was my answer. Does the title please you, my dear Henry?"

"Hem! I don't think the title promises anything particularly fine. But, never mind; go on! If it does not please us, we will stop you, and you must begin another; and so on, I can tell you, until you really do fix upon a good one."

"One moment!" I exclaimed. "I will not accept those conditions. If you were grown-up persons, well and good!"

"Nevertheless, those are our conditions: if not, a prisoner you must remain with us for ever."

"My dear Henry, you are a charming boy—well brought up—and I shall be much surprised if you do not some day become Prime Minister of England. Let me go free, and I will do all you ask."

"On your word of honour?"

"On my word of honour."

At the same moment I felt the thousand threads that held me suddenly become loose: each of the little tormentors had set to work to untie a knot; and in half a minute I was at liberty.

Now as every one must keep his word, even when it is pledged to children, I desired my audience to sit round me; and when the children had all placed themselves in a manner so comfortable that I fancied they would soon fall off to sleep in their chairs, I began my story in the following manner.

Godfather Drosselmayer

Once upon a time there lived at Nuremberg, in Germany, a judge of great respectability, and who was called Judge Silberhaus, which means "silver-house."

This judge had a son and daughter. The son was nine years old, and was named Fritz: the daughter, who was seven and a half, was called Mary.

They were two beautiful children; but so different in disposition and features, that no one would have believed them to be brother and sister.

Fritz was a fine stout boy with ruddy cheeks and roguish looks. He was very impatient, and stamped on the floor whenever he was contradicted; for he thought that everything in the world had been made for his amusement, or to suit his fancy. In this humour he would remain until the judge, annoyed by his cries and screams, or by his stamping, came out of his study, and, raising his forefinger, said with a frown, "Master Fritz!"

These two words were quite sufficient to make Master Fritz wish that the earth would open and swallow him up.

As for his mother, it was no matter how much or how often she raised her fore-finger; for Fritz did not mind her at all.

His sister Mary was, on the contrary, a delicate and pale child, with long hair curling naturally, and flowing over her little white shoulders like a flood of golden light upon a vase of alabaster. She was sweet, amiable, bashful, and kind to all who were in sorrow, even to her dolls: she was very obedient to her mamma, and never contradicted her governess, Miss Trudchen; so that Mary was beloved by every one.

Now, the 24th of December, 17. . ., had arrived. You all know, my dear young friends, that the 24th of December is called Christmas Eve, being the day before the one on which the Redeemer Jesus was born.

But I must now explain something to you. You have all heard, perhaps, that every country has its peculiar customs; and the best read amongst you are aware that Nuremberg, in Germany, is a town famous for its toys, puppets, and playthings, of which it exports great quantities to other countries. You will admit, therefore, that the little boys and girls of Nuremberg ought to be the happiest children in the world, unless, indeed, they are like the inhabitants of Ostend, who seem only to delight in their oysters for the purpose of sending them to foreign markets. Germany, being quite a different country from England, has altogether other customs. In England, New Year's Day is the grand day for making presents, so that many parents would be very glad if the year always commenced with the 2nd of January.

But in Germany the great day for presents is the 24th of December, the one preceding Christmas Day. Moreover, in Germany, children's presents are given in a peculiar way. A large shrub is placed upon a table in the drawing-room; and to all its branches are hung the toys to be distributed among the children. Such playthings as are too heavy to hang to the shrub, are placed on the table; and the children are then told that it is their guardian angel who sends them all those pretty toys. This is a very innocent deception, after all; and perhaps it can scarcely be called a deception, because all the good things of this world are sent to us by heaven.

I need scarcely tell you that among those children of Nuremberg who received most presents were the son and daughter of Judge Silberhaus; for besides their father and mother, who doted on them, they also had a godfather who loved them dearly, and whose name was Drosselmayer.

I must describe in a few words the portrait of this illustrious person, who occupied in the town of Nuremberg a position almost as high as that of Judge Silberhaus himself.

Godfather Drosselmayer, who was a great physician and doctor of medicine, was by no means a very good-looking person. He was a tall thin man, about six feet high, but who stooped very much, so that, in spite of the length of his legs, he could almost pick up his handkerchief, if it fell, without stooping any lower. His face was wrinkled as a golden rennet that has withered and fallen from the tree. Being blind of the right eye, he wore a black patch; and, being entirely bald, he wore a shining and frizzled wig, which he had made himself with spun glass, such as you may have seen the glass-blowers spin at the Adelaide Gallery or Polytechnic Institution. He was, however, compelled, for fear of damaging this ingenious contrivance, to carry his hat under his arm. His remaining eye was sparkling and bright, and seemed not only to perform its own duty, but that of its absent companion, so rapidly did it glance round any room which Godfather Drosselmayer was desirous to scrutinize in all points, or fix upon any person whose secret thoughts he wished to read.

Now, Godfather Drosselmayer, who was a learned doctor, did not follow the example of those physicians who allow their patients to die, but occupied his time in giving life to dead things: I mean that, by studying the formation of men and animals, he had gained so deep a knowledge of the manner in which they are made, that he was able to manufacture men who could walk, bow to each other, and go through their exercises with a musket. He also made ladies who danced, and played upon the harpsichord, the harp, and the viol; dogs that ran, carried, and barked; birds that flew, hopped, and sang; and fish that swam, and ate crumbs of bread. He had even succeeded in making puppets and images of Punch utter a few words—not many, it is true, but such as "papa," "mamma," &c. The tones were certainly harsh, and always the same in sound; because you can very well understand that all this was done merely by means of machinery concealed inside the toys; and no machinery can ever perform the same wonders as the beings which God has created.

Nevertheless, in spite of all difficulties, Godfather Drosselmayer did not despair of being some day able to make real men, real women, real dogs, real birds, and real fish. It is scarcely necessary to add that his two godchildren, to whom he had promised the first proofs of his success in this line, awaited the happy moment with great impatience.

Godfather Drosselmayer, having reached this state of perfection in mechanical science, was a most useful man to his friends. Thus, for instance, if a time-piece at the house of Judge Silberhaus got out of order, in spite of the attentions of the usual clock-makers—if the hands suddenly stopped—if the tick-tick seemed to go badly—or if the wheels inside would not move—Godfather Drosselmayer was immediately sent for; and he hastened to the house as quick as he could, for he was a man devoted to the art of mechanics. He was no sooner shown the poor clock, than he instantly opened it, took out the works, and placed them between his knees. Then, with his eye glittering like a carbuncle, and his wig laid upon the floor, he drew from his pocket a number of little tools which he had made himself, and the proper use of which he alone knew. Choosing the most pointed one, he plunged it into the very midst of the works, to the great alarm of little Mary, who could not believe that the poor clock did not suffer from the operation. But in a short time when the old gentleman had touched the works in various parts, and placed them again in their case, or on their stand, or between the four pillars of the time-piece, as the case might be, the clock soon began to revive, to tick as loud as ever, and to strike with its shrill clear voice at the proper time; a circumstance that gave new life, as it were, to the room itself, which without it seemed a melancholy place.

Moreover, in compliance with the wishes of little Mary, who was grieved to see the kitchen dog turning the spit, Godfather Drosselmayer made a wooden dog, which by means of mechanism connected inside, turned the spit without annoyance to itself. Turk, who had done this duty for three years, until he had become quite shaky all over, was now able to lie down in peace in front of the kitchen fire, and amuse himself by watching the movements of his successor.

Thus, after the judge, after the judge's wife, after Fritz, and after Mary, the dog Turk was certainly the next inmate of the house who had most reason to love and respect Godfather Drosselmayer. Turk was indeed grateful, and showed his joy, whenever Drosselmayer drew near the house, by leaping up against the front door and wagging his tail, even before the old gentleman had knocked.

On the evening of the 24th of December, just as the twilight was approaching, Fritz and Mary, who had not been allowed to enter the drawing-room all day, were huddled together in a corner of the dining-parlour. Miss Trudchen, the governess, was knitting near the window, to which she had moved her chair, in order to catch the last rays of day-light. The children were seized with a kind of vague fear, because candles had not been brought into the room, according to custom; so they were talking in a low tone to each other, just as children talk when they are afraid.

"Fritz," said Mary, "I am sure papa and mamma are busy in preparing the Christmas tree; for ever since the morning I have heard a great deal going on in the drawing-room, which we were forbidden to enter."

"And I know," said Fritz, "by the way Turk barked ten minutes ago, that Godfather Drosselmayer has arrived."

"Oh! I wonder what our dear kind godfather has brought us!" exclaimed Mary, clapping her little hands. "I am sure it will be a beautiful garden, planted with trees, and with a beautiful river running between the banks, covered with flowers. And on the river, too, there will be some silver swans with collars of gold, and a little girl will bring them sweet-cake, which they will eat out of her apron."

"In the first place, Miss," said Fritz, in that authoritative tone which was natural to him, and which his parents considered to be one of his greatest faults, "you must know that swans do not eat sweet-cake."

"I thought they did," answered Mary; "but as you are a year and a half older than I, you must know best."

Fritz tossed his head up with an air of importance.

"And, for my part," he continued, "I feel certain that if Godfather Drosselmayer brings anything at all, it will be a castle with soldiers to watch it, and enemies to attack it. We shall then have some famous battles."

"I do not like battles," said Mary. "If he does bring a castle, as you think he will, it must be for you: I shall, however, take care of the wounded."

"Whatever it is that he brings," returned Fritz, "you know very well that it is neither for you nor for me; because the toys which Godfather Drosselmayer gives us are always taken away again immediately afterwards, under pretence that they really are works of great art. Then, you know, they are always put into that great cupboard with the glass doors, and on the top shelves, which papa himself can only reach when he stands upon a chair. So, after all, I much prefer the toys which papa and mamma give us, and which we are allowed to play with until we break them into a thousand pieces."

"And so do I," answered Mary; "only we must not say so to godfather."

"And why not?"

"Because he would feel annoyed to think that we do not like his toys as much as those which papa and mamma give us. He gives them to us, thinking to please us; and it would be wrong to tell him the contrary."

"Oh! nonsense," cried Fritz.

"Miss Mary is quite right, Master Fritz," said Dame Trudchen, who was generally very silent, and only spoke on important occasions.

"Come," said Mary hastily, in order to prevent Fritz from giving an impudent answer to the poor governess; "let us guess what our parents intend to give us. For my part I told mamma—but upon condition that she would not scold—that Miss Rose, my doll, grows more and more awkward, in spite of the lessons which I am constantly giving her; and that she does nothing but fall upon her nose, which never fails to leave most disagreeable marks upon her face; so that I can no longer take her into decent society, because her face does not at all correspond with her frocks."

"And I," said Fritz, "did not hesitate to assure papa that a nice little horse would look admirably well in my stables;

I also took the opportunity to inform him that no army can possibly exist without cavalry, and that I want a squadron of hussars to complete the division which I command."

These words made Miss Trudchen conclude that the moment was favourable for her to speak a second time.

"Master Fritz and Miss Mary," said she, "you know very well that it is your guardian angel who sends and blesses all those fine toys which are given to you. Do not therefore say beforehand what you want; because the angel knows much better than you what will please you."

"Oh!" cried Fritz; "and yet last year he sent me foot soldiers, although, as I have just said, I should have been better satisfied with a squadron of hussars."

"For my part I have only to thank my good angel," said Mary; "for did I but ask for a doll last year, and I not only had the doll, but also a beautiful white dove with red feet and beak."

In the meantime the night had altogether drawn in, and the children, who by degrees spoke lower and lower, and grew closer and closer together, fancied that they heard the wings of their guardian angels fluttering near them, and a sweet music in the distance, like that of an organ accompanying the Hymn of the Nativity, beneath the gloomy arches of a cathedral. Presently a sudden light shone upon the wall for a moment, and Fritz and Mary believed that it was their guardian angel, who, after depositing the toys in the drawing-room, flew away in the midst of a golden lustre to visit other children who were expecting him with the same impatience as themselves.

Immediately afterward a bell rang—the door was thrown violently open—and so strong a light burst into the apartment that the children were dazzled, and uttered cries of surprise and alarm.

The judge and his wife then appeared at the door, and took the hands of their children, saying, "Come, little dears, and see what the guardian angels have sent you."

The children hastened to the drawing-room; and Miss Trudchen, having placed her work upon a chair, followed them.

THE CHRISTMAS TREE

My dear children, you all know the beautiful toy-stalls in the Soho Bazaar, the Pantheon, and the Lowther Arcade; and your parents have often taken you there, to permit you to choose whatever you liked best. Then you have stopped short, with longing eyes and open mouth; and you have experienced a pleasure which you will never again know in your lives—no, not even when you become men and acquire titles or fortunes. Well, the same joy was felt by Fritz and Mary when they entered the drawing-room and saw the great tree growing as it were from the middle of the table, and covered with blossoms made of sugar, and sugar-plums instead of fruit—the whole glittering by the light of a hundred Christmas candles concealed amidst the leaves. At the beautiful sight Fritz leapt for joy, and danced about in a manner which showed how well he had attended to the lessons of his dancing-master. On her side, Mary could not restrain two large tears of joy which, like liquid pearls, rolled down her countenance, that was open and smiling as a rose in June. But the children's joy knew no bounds when they came to examine all the pretty things which covered the table. There was a beautiful doll, twice as large as Miss Rose; and there was also a charming silk frock, hung on a stand in such a manner that Mary could walk around it. Fritz was also well pleased; for he found upon the table a squadron of hussars, with red jackets and gold lace, and mounted on white horses; while on the carpet, near the table, stood the famous horse which he also much longed to see in his stables. In a moment did this modern Alexander leap upon the back of that brilliant Bucephalus, which was already saddled and bridled; and, having ridden two or three times around the table, he got off again, declaring that though the animal was very spirited and restive, he should soon be able to tame him in such a manner that ere a month passed the horse would be quiet as a lamb.

But at the moment when Fritz set his foot upon the ground, and when Mary was baptising her new doll by the name of Clara, the bell rang a second time; and the children turned towards that corner of the room when the sound came.

They then beheld something which had hitherto escaped their attention, so intent had they been upon the beautiful Christmas tree. In fact, the corner of the room of which I have just spoken, was concealed, or cut off as it were, by a large Chinese screen, behind which there was a certain noise accompanied by a certain sweet music, which proved that something unusual was going on in that quarter. The children then recollected that they had not yet seen the doctor; and they both exclaimed at the same moment, "Oh! Godpapa Drosselmayer!"

At these words—and as if it had only waited for that exclamation to put itself in motion—the screen opened inwards, and showed not only Godfather Drosselmayer, but something more!

In the midst of a green meadow, decorated with flowers, stood a magnificent country-seat, with numerous windows, all made of real glass, in front, and two gilt towers on the wings. At the same moment the jingling of bells was heard from within—the doors and windows opened—and the rooms inside were discovered lighted up by wax-tapers half an inch high. In those rooms were several little gentlemen and ladies, all walking about: the gentlemen splendidly dressed in laced coats, and silk waistcoats and breeches, each with a sword by his side, and a hat under his arm; the ladies gorgeously attired in brocades, their hair dressed in the style of the eighteenth century, and each one holding a fan in her hand, wherewith they all fanned themselves as if overcome by the heat. In the central drawing-room, which actually seemed to be on fire, so splendid was the lustre of the crystal chandelier, filled with wax candles, a number of children were dancing to the jingling music; the boys all in round jackets, and the girls all in short frocks. At the same time a gentleman, clad in a furred cloak, appeared at the window of an adjoining chamber, made signs, and then disappeared again; while Godfather Drosselmayer himself, with his drab frock-coat, the patch on his eye, and the glass wig—so like the original, although only three inches high, that the puppet might be taken for the doctor, as if seen at a great distance—went out and in the front door of the mansion with the air of a gentleman, inviting those who were walking outside to enter his abode.

The first moment was one of surprise and delight for the two children; but, having watched the building for a few minutes with his elbows resting on the table, Fritz rose and exclaimed, "But, Godpapa Drosselmayer, why do you keep going out and coming in by the same door? You must be tired of going backward and forward like that. Come, enter by that door there, and come out by this one here."

And Fritz pointed with his finger to the doors of the two towers.

"No, that cannot be done," answered Godfather Drosselmayer.

"Well, then," said Fritz, "do me the pleasure of going up those stairs, and taking the place of that gentleman at the window: then tell him to go down to the door."

"It is impossible, my dear Fritz," again said the doctor.

"At all events the children have danced enough: let them go and walk, while the gentlemen and ladies who are now walking, dance in their turn."

"But you are not reasonable, you little rogue," cried the godpapa, who began to grow angry: "the mechanism must move in a certain way."

"Then let me go into the house," said Fritz.

"Now you are silly, my dear boy," observed the judge: "you see that it is impossible for you to enter the house, since the vanes on the top of the towers scarcely come up to your shoulders."

Fritz yielded to this reasoning and held his tongue; but in a few moments, seeing that the ladies and gentlemen kept on walking, that the children would not leave off dancing, that the gentleman with the furred cloak appeared and disappeared at regular intervals, and that Godfather Drosselmayer did not leave the door, he again broke his silence.

"My dear godpapa," said he, "if all these little figures can do nothing more than what they are doing over and over again, you may take them away to-morrow, for I do not care about them; and I like my horse much better,

because it runs when I choose—and my hussars, because they manœuvre at my command, and wheel to the right or left, or march forward or backward, and are not shut up in any house like your poor little people who can only move over and over in the same way.

With these words he turned his back upon Godfather Drosselmayer and the house, hastened to the table, and drew up his hussars in battle array.

As for Mary, she had slipped away very gently, because the motions of the little figures in the house seemed to her to be very tiresome: but as she was a charming child, she said nothing, for fear of wounding the feelings of Godpapa Drosselmayer. Indeed, the moment Fritz turned his back, the doctor said to the judge and his wife, in a tone of vexation, "This master-piece is not fit for children; and I will put my house back again into the box, and take it away."

But the judge's wife approached him, and, in order to atone for her son's rudeness, begged Godfather Drosselmayer to explain to her all the secrets of the beautiful house, and praised the ingenuity of the mechanism to such an extent, that she not only made the doctor forget his vexation, but put him into such a good humour, that he drew from the pockets of his drab coat a number of little men and women with horn complexions, white eyes, and gilt hands and feet. Besides the beauty of their appearance, these little men and women set forth a delicious perfume, because they were made of cinnamon.

At this moment Miss Trudchen called Mary, and offered to help her to put on the pretty little silk frock which she had so much admired on first entering the drawing-room; but Mary, in spite of her usual politeness, did not answer the governess, so much was she occupied with a new personage whom she had discovered amongst the toys, and to whom, my dear children, I must briefly direct your attention, since he is actually the hero of my tale, in which Miss Trudchen, Mary, Fritz, the judge, the judge's lady, and even Godfather Drosselmayer, are only secondary characters.

The Little Man with the Wooden Cloak

I told you that Mary did not reply to the invitation of Miss Trudchen, because she had just discovered a new toy which she had not before perceived.

Indeed, by dint of making his hussars march and counter-march about the table, Fritz had brought to light a charming little gentleman, who, leaning in a melancholy mood against the trunk of the Christmas tree, awaited, in silence and polite reserve, the moment when his turn to be inspected should arrive. We must pause to notice the appearance of this little man, to whom I gave the epithet "charming" somewhat hastily; for, in addition to his body being too long and large for the miserable little thin legs which supported it, his head was of a size so enormous that it was quite at variance with the proportions indicated not only by nature, but also by those drawing-masters who know much better than even Nature herself.

But if there were any fault in his person, that defect was atoned for by the excellence of his toilette, which denoted at once a man of education and taste. He wore a braided frock-coat of violet-coloured velvet, all frogged and covered with buttons; trousers of the same material; and the most charming little Wellington boots ever seen on the feet of a student or an officer. But these were two circumstances which seemed strange in respect to a man who preserved such elegant taste: the one was an ugly narrow cloak made of wood, and which hung down like a pig's tale from the nape of his neck to the middle of his back; and the other was a wretched cap, such as peasants sometimes wear in Switzerland, upon his head. But Mary, when she perceived those two objects which seemed so unsuitable to the rest of the costume, remembered that Godfather Drosselmayer himself wore above his drab coat a little collar of no better appearance than the wooden cloak belonging to the little gentleman in the military frock; and that the doctor often covered his own bald head with an ugly—an absolutely frightful cap, unlike all other ugly caps in the world—although this circumstance did not prevent the doctor from being an excellent godpapa. She even thought to herself that were Godpapa Drosselmayer to imitate altogether the dress of the little gentleman with the wooden cloak, he could not possibly become so genteel and interesting as the puppet.

You can very well believe that these reflections on the part of Mary were not made without a close inspection of the little man, whom she liked from the very first moment that she saw him. Then, the more she looked at him, the more she was struck by the sweetness and amiability which were expressed by his countenance. His clear green eyes, which were certainly rather goggle, beamed with serenity and kindness. The frizzled beard of white cotton, extending beneath his chin, seemed to become him amazingly, because it set off the charming smile of his mouth, which was rather wide perhaps; but then, the lips were as red as vermilion!

Thus was it that, after examining the little man for upwards of ten minutes, without daring to touch it, Mary exclaimed, "Oh! dear papa, whose is that funny figure leaning against the Christmas tree?"

"It belongs to no one in particular," answered the judge; "but to both of you together."

"How do you mean, dear papa? I do not understand you."

"This little man," continued the judge, "will help you both; for it is he who in future will crack all your nuts for you; and he belongs as much to Fritz as to you, and as much to you as Fritz."

Thus speaking, the judge took up the little man very carefully, and raising his wood cloak, made him open his mouth by a very simple motion, and display two rows of sharp white teeth. Mary then placed a nut in the little man's mouth; and crack—crack—the shell was broken into a dozen pieces, and the kernel fell whole and sound into Mary's hand. The little girl then learnt that the dandified gentleman belonged to that ancient and respectable race of Nutcrackers whose origin is as ancient as that of the town of Nuremberg, and that he continued to exercise the honourable calling of his forefathers. Mary, delighted to have made this discovery, leapt for joy; whereupon the judge said, "Well, my dear little Mary, since the Nutcracker pleases you so much, although it belongs equally to Fritz and yourself, it is to you that I especially trust it. I place it in your care."

With these words the judge handed the little fellow to Mary, who took the puppet in her arms, and began to practise it in its vocation, choosing, however—so good was her heart—the smallest nuts, that it might not be compelled to open its mouth too wide, because by so doing its face assumed a most ridiculous expression. Then Miss Trudchen drew near to behold the little puppet in her turn; and for her also did it perform its duty in the most unassuming and obliging manner in the world, although she was but a dependant.

While he was employed in training his horse and parading his Hussars, Master Fritz heard the crack—crack so often repeated, that he felt sure something new was going on. He accordingly looked up and turned his large inquiring eyes upon the group composed of the judge, Mary, and Miss Trudchen; and when he observed the little man with the wooden cloak in his sister's arms, he leapt from his horse, and, without waiting to put the animal in its stable, hastened towards Mary. Then what a joyous shout of laughter burst from his lips as he espied the funny appearance of the little man opening his large mouth. Fritz also demanded his share of the nuts which the puppet cracked; and this was of course granted. Next he wanted to hold the little man while he cracked the nuts; and this wish was also gratified. Only, in spite of the remonstrances of his sister, Fritz chose the largest and hardest nuts to cram into his mouth; so that at the fifth or sixth c-r-r-ack! and out fell three of the poor little fellow's teeth. At the same time his chin fell and became tremulous like that of an old man.

"Oh! my poor Nutcracker!" ejaculated Mary, snatching the little man from the hands of Fritz.

"What a stupid fellow he is!" cried the boy: "he pretends to be a Nutcracker, and his jaws are as brittle as 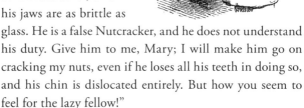 glass. He is a false Nutcracker, and he does not understand his duty. Give him to me, Mary; I will make him go on cracking my nuts, even if he loses all his teeth in doing so, and his chin is dislocated entirely. But how you seem to feel for the lazy fellow!"

"No—no—no!" cried Mary, clasping the little man in her arms: "no—you shall not have my Nutcracker! See how he looks at me, as much as to tell me that his poor jaw is hurt. Fie, Fritz! you are very ill-natured—you beat your horses; and the other day you shot one of your soldiers."

"I beat my horses when they are restive," said Fritz, with an air of importance; "and as for the soldier whom I shot the other day, he was a wretched scoundrel that I never have been able to do anything with for the last year, and who deserted one fine morning with his arms and baggage—a crime that is punishable by death in all countries. Besides, all these things are matters of discipline which do not regard women. I do not prevent you from boxing your doll's ears; so don't try to hinder me from whipping my horses or shooting my soldiers. But I want the Nutcracker."

"Papa—papa!—help—help!" cried Mary, wrapping the little man in her pocket-handkerchief: "help! Fritz is going to take the Nutcracker from me!"

At Mary's cries, not only the judge drew near the children; but his wife and Godfather Drosselmayer also ran towards them. The two children told their stories in their own way—Mary wishing to keep the Nutcracker, and Fritz anxious to have it again. But to the astonishment of Mary, Godfather Drosselmayer, with a smile that seemed perfectly frightful to the poor little girl, decided in favor of Fritz. Happily for the poor Nutcracker, the judge and his wife took little Mary's part.

"My dear Fritz," said the judge, "I trusted the Nutcracker to the care of your sister; and as far as my knowledge of surgery goes, I see that the poor creature is unwell and requires attention. I therefore give him over solely to the care of Mary, until he is quite well; and no one must say a word against my decision. And you, Fritz, who stand up so firmly in behalf of military discipline, when did you ever hear of making a wounded soldier return to his duty? The wounded always go to the hospital until they are cured; and if they be disabled by their wounds, they are entitled to pensions."

Fritz was about to reply; but the judge raised his fore-finger to a level with his right eye, and said, "Master Fritz!"

You have already seen what influence those two words had upon the little boy: thus, ashamed at having drawn upon himself the reprimand conveyed in those words, he slipped quietly off, without giving any answer, to the table where his hussars were posted: then, having placed the sentinels in their stations, he marched off the rest to their quarters for the night.

In the meantime Mary picked up the three little teeth which had fallen from the Nutcracker's mouth, and kept the Nutcracker himself well wrapped up in the pocket-handkerchief; she had also bound up his chin with a pretty white ribbon which she cut from the frock. On his side, the little man, who was at first very pale and much frightened, seemed quite con-tented in the care of his protectress, and gradually acquired confidence, when he felt himself gently rocked in her arms. Then Mary perceived that Godfather Drosselmayer watched with mocking smiles the care which she bestowed upon the little man with the wooden cloak; and it struck her that the single eye of the doctor had acquired an expression of spite and malignity which she had never before seen. She therefore tried to get away from him; but Godfather Drosselmayer burst out laughing, saying, "Well, my dear goddaughter, I am really astonished that a pretty girl like you can be so devoted to an ugly little urchin like that."

Mary turned round; and much as she loved her god-father, even the compliment which he paid her did not make amends for the unjust attack he made upon the person of her Nutcracker. She even felt—contrary to her usual disposition—very angry; and that vague comparison which she had before formed between the little man with the wooden cloak and her godfather, returned to her memory.

"Godpapa Drosselmayer," she said, "you are unkind towards my little Nutcracker, whom you call an ugly urchin. Who knows whether you would even look so well as he, even if you had his pretty little military coat, his pretty little breeches, and his pretty little boots!"

At these words Mary's parents burst out laughing; and the doctor's nose grew prodigiously longer.

Why did the doctor's nose grow so much longer? Mary, surprised by the effect of her remark, could not guess the reason.

But there are never any effects without causes, that reason no doubt belonged to some strange and unknown cause, which we must explain.

WONDERFUL EVENTS

I do not know, my dear little friends, whether you remember that I spoke of a certain large cupboard, with glass windows, in which the children's toys were locked up. This cupboard was on the right side of the door of the judge's own room. Mary was still a baby in the cradle, and Fritz had only just begun to walk, when the judge had that cupboard made by a very skilful carpenter, who put such brilliant glass in the frames, that the toys appeared a thousand times finer when ranged on the shelves than when they were held in the hand. Upon the top shelf of all, which neither Fritz nor Mary could reach, the beautiful pieces of workmanship of Godfather Drosselmayer were placed. Immediately beneath was the shelf containing the picture-books; and the two lower shelves were given to Fritz and Mary, who filled them in the way they liked best. It seemed, however, to have been tacitly agreed upon between the two children, that Fritz should hold possession of the higher shelf of the two, for the marshalling of his troops, and that Mary should keep the lower shelf for her dolls and their households. This arrangement was entered into on the eve of Christmas Day. Fritz placed his soldiers upon his own shelf; and Mary, having thrust Miss Rose into a corner, gave the bed-room, formed by the lowest shelf, to Miss Clara, with whom she invited herself to pass the evening and enjoy a supper of sugar-plums. Miss Clara, on casting her eyes around, saw that everything was in proper order; her table well spread with sugar-plums and conserved fruits, and her nice white bed with its white counterpane, all so neat and comfortable. She therefore felt very well satisfied with her new apartment.

While all these arrangements were being made, the evening wore away: midnight was approaching—Godfather Drosselmayer had been gone a long time—and yet the children could not be persuaded to quit the cupboard.

Contrary to custom, it was Fritz that yielded first to the persuasion of his parents, who told him that it was time to go to bed.

"Well," said he, "after all the exercise which my poor hussars have had to-day, they must be fatigued; and as those excellent soldiers all know their duty towards me—and as, so long as I remain here, they will not close their eyes—I must retire."

With these words—and having given them the watch-word, to prevent them from being surprised by a patrol of the enemy—Fritz went off to bed.

But this was not the case with Mary; and as her mamma, who was about to follow her husband to their bed-chamber, desired her to tear herself away from the dearly-beloved cupboard, little Mary said, "Only one moment, dear mamma—a single moment: do let me finish all I have to do here. There are a hundred or more important things to put to rights; and the moment I have settled them, I promise to go to bed."

Mary requested this favour in so touching and plaintive a tone—she was, moreover, so glad and obedient a child—that her mother did not hesitate to grant her request. Nevertheless, as Miss Trudchen had already gone up stairs to get Mary's bed ready, the judge's wife, thinking that her daughter might forget to put out the candles, performed that duty herself, leaving only a light in the lamp hanging from the ceiling.

"Do not be long before you go to your room, dear little Mary," said the judge's wife; for if you remain up too long, you will not be able to rise at your usual hour to-morrow morning."

With these words the lady quitted the room and closed the door behind her.

The moment Mary found herself alone, she bethought herself, above all things, of her poor little Nutcracker; for she contrived to keep it in her arms, wrapped up in her pocket handkerchief. She placed him upon the table very gently, unrolled her handkerchief, and examined his chin. The Nutcracker still seemed to suffer much pain, and appeared very cross.

"Ah! my dear little fellow," she said in a low tone, "do not be angry, I pray, because my brother Fritz hurt you so much. He had no evil intention, rest well assured; only his manners have become rough, and his heart is a little hardened by his soldier's life. Otherwise he is a very good boy, I can assure you; and I know that when you are better acquainted with him, you will forgive him. Besides, to atone for the injury which he has done you, I will take care of you; which I will do so attentively that in a few days you will be quite well. As for putting in the teeth again and fastening your chin properly, that is the business of

Godpapa Drosselmayer, who perfectly understands those kinds of things."

Mary could say no more; for the moment she pronounced the name of her Godfather Drosselmayer, the Nutcracker, to whom this discourse was addressed, made so dreadful a grimace, and his eyes suddenly flashed so brightly, that the little girl stopped short in affright, and stepped a pace back. But as the Nutcracker immediately afterwards resumed its amiable expression and its melancholy smile, she fancied that she must have been the sport of an illusion, and that the flame of the lamp, agitated by a current of air, had thus disfigured the little man. She even laughed at herself, saying, "I am indeed very foolish to think that this wooden puppet could make faces to me. Come, let me draw near the poor fellow, and take that care of him which he requires."

Having thus mused within herself, Mary took the puppet once more in her arms, drew near the cupboard, knocked at the glass door, which Fritz had closed, and said to the new doll, "I beg of you, Miss Clara, to give up your bed to my poor Nutcracker, who is unwell, and to shift for yourself on the sofa to-night. Remember that you are in excellent health yourself, as your round and rosy cheeks sufficiently prove. Moreover, a night is soon passed; the sofa is very comfortable, and there will not be many dolls in Nuremberg as well lodged as yourself."

Miss Clara, as you may well suppose, did not utter a word; but it struck Mary that she seemed very sulky and discontented; but Mary, whose conscience told her that she had treated Miss Clara in the most considerate manner, used no further ceremony with her, but, drawing the bed towards her, placed the Nutcracker in it, covering him with the clothes up to the very chin: she then thought that she knew nothing as yet of the real disposition of Miss Clara, whom she had only seen for a few hours; but that as Miss Clara had appeared to be in a very bad humour at losing her bed, some evil might happen to the poor invalid if he were left with so insolent a person. She therefore placed the bed, with the Nutcracker in it, upon the second shelf, close by the ridge where Fritz's cavalry were quartered: then, having laid Miss Clara upon the sofa, she closed the cupboard, and was about to rejoin Miss Trudchen in the bed-chamber, when all around the room the poor girl heard a variety of low scratching sounds coming from behind the chairs, the store, and the cupboard. The large clock which hung against the wall, and which was surmounted by a large gilt owl, instead of a cuckoo, as is usual with old German clocks, began that usual whirring sound which gives warning of striking; and yet it did not strike. Mary glanced towards it, and saw that the immense gilt owl had drooped its wings in such a way that they covered the entire clock, and that the bird thrust forward as far as it could its hideous cat-like head, with the round eyes and the crooked beak. Then the whirring sound of the clock became louder and louder, and gradually changed into the resemblance of a human voice, until it appeared as if these words issued from the beak of the owl: "Clocks, clocks, clocks! whir, whir, whir! in a low tone! The king of the mice has a sharp ear! Sing him his old song! Strike, strike, strike, clocks all: sound his last hour—for his fate is nigh at hand!"

And then, dong—dong—dong—the clock struck twelve in a hollow and gloomy tone.

Mary was very much frightened. She began to shudder from head to foot; and she was about to run away from the room, when she beheld Godfather Drosselmayer seated upon the clock instead of the owl, the two skirts of his coat having taken the place of the drooping wings of the bird. At that spectacle, Mary remained nailed as it were to the spot with astonishment; and she began to cry, saying, "What are you doing up there, Godpapa Drosselmayer?

Come down here, and don't frighten me like that, naughty Godpapa Drosselmayer."

But at these words there began a sharp whistling and furious kind of tittering all around: then in a few moments Mary heard thousands of little feet treading behind the walls; and next she saw thousands of little lights through the joints in the wainscot. When I say little lights, I am wrong—I mean thousands of little eyes. Mary full well perceived that there was an entire population of mice about to enter the room. And, in fact, in the course of five minutes, thousands and thousands of mice made their appearance by the creases of the door and the joints of the floor, and began to gallop hither and thither, until at length they ranged themselves in order of battle, as Fritz was wont to draw upon his wood soldiers. All this seemed very amusing to Mary; and as she did not feel towards mice that absurd alarm which so many foolish children experience, she thought she should divert herself with the sight, when there suddenly rang through the room a whistling so sharp, so terrible, and so long, that a cold shudder passed over her.

At the same time, a plank was raised up by some power underneath, and the king of the mice, with seven heads all wearing gold crowns, appeared at her very feet, in the midst of the mortar and plaster that was broken up; and each of his seven mouths began to whistle and scream horribly, while the body to which those seven heads belonged forced its way through the opening. The entire army advanced towards the king, speaking with their little mouths three times in chorus. Then the various regiments marched across the room, directing their course towards the cupboard, and surrounding Mary on all sides, so that she began to beat a retreat. I have already told you that Mary was not a timid child; but when she saw herself surrounded by crowds of mice, commanded by that monster with seven heads, fear seized upon her, and her heart began to beat so violently, that it seemed as if it would burst from her chest. Her blood appeared to freeze in her veins, her breath failed her; and, half fainting, she retreated with trembling steps. At length—pir-r-r-r! and the pieces of the panes in the cupboard, broken by her elbow which knocked against it, fell upon the floor. She felt at the moment an acute pain in the left arm; but at the same time her heart grew lighter, for she no longer heard that squeaking which had so much frightened her. Indeed, everything had again become quiet around her; the mice had disappeared; and she thought that, terrified by the noises of the glass which was broken, they had sought refuge in their holes.

But almost immediately afterwards a strange noise commenced in the cupboard; and numerous little sharp voices exclaimed, "To arms! to arms! to arms!" At the same time the music of Godfather Drosselmayer's country-house, which had been placed upon the top shelf of the cupboard, began to play; and on all sides she heard the words, "Quick! rise to arms! to arms!"

Mary turned round. The cupboard was lighted up in a wondrous manner, and all was bustle within. All the harlequins, the clowns, the punches, and the other puppets scampered about; while the dolls set to work to make lint and prepare bandages for the wounded. At length the Nutcracker himself threw off all the clothes, and jumped off the bed, crying, "Foolish troop of mice! return to your holes, or you must encounter me!"

But at that menace a loud whistling echoed through the room; and Mary perceived that the mice had not returned to their holes; but that, frightened by the noise of the broken glass, they had sought refuge beneath the chairs and tables, whence they were now beginning to issue again.

On his side, Nutcracker, far from being terrified by the whistling, seemed to gather fresh courage.

"Despicable king of the mice," he exclaimed; "it is thou, then! Thou acceptest the death which I have so long offered you? Come on, and let this night decide between us. And you, my good friends—my companions—my brethren, if it be indeed true that we are united in bonds of affection, support me in this perilous contest! On! on!— let those who love me follow!"

Never did a proclamation produce such an effect. Two harlequins, a clown, two punches, and three other puppets, cried out in a loud tone, "Yes, my lord, we are yours in life and death! We will conquer under your command, or die with you!"

At these words, which proved that there was an echo to his speech in the heart of his friends, Nutcracker felt himself so excited, that he drew his sword, and without calculating the dreadful height on which he stood, leapt from the second shelf. Mary, upon perceiving that dangerous leap, gave a piercing cry; for Nutcracker seemed on the point of being dashed to pieces; when Miss Clara, who was on the lower shelf, darted from the sofa and received him in her arms.

"Ah! my dear little Clara," said Mary, clasping her hands together with emotion: "how have I mistaken your disposition!"

But Miss Clara, thinking only of the present events, said to the Nutcracker, "What! my lord—wounded and suffering as you are, you are plunging headlong into new dangers! Content yourself with commanding the army, and let the others fight. Your courage is known; and you can do no good by giving fresh proof of it!"

And as she spoke, Clara endeavoured to restrain the gallant Nutcracker by holding him tight in her arms; but he began to struggle and kick in such a manner that Miss Clara was obliged to let him glide down. He slipped from her arms, and fell on his knees at her feet in a most graceful manner, saying, "Princess, believe me, that although at a certain period you were unjust towards me, I shall always remember you, even in the midst of battle!"

Miss Clara stooped as low down as possible, and, taking him by his little arm, compelled him to rise: then taking off her waist-band all glittering with spangles, she made a scarf of it, and sought to pass it over the shoulder of the young hero; but he, stepping back a few paces, and bowing at the same time in acknowledgment of so great a favour, untied the little white ribbon with which Mary had bound up his chin, and tied it round his waist, after pressing it to his lips. Then, light as a bird, he leapt from the shelf on the floor, brandishing his sabre all the time. Immediately did the squeakings and creakings of the mice begin over again; and the king of the mice, as if to reply to the challenge of the Nutcracker, issued from beneath the great table in the middle of the room, followed by the main body of his army. At the same time, the wings, on the right and left, began to appear from beneath the arm-chair, under which they had taken refuge.

The Battle

"Trumpets, sound the charge! drums, beat the alarm!" exclaimed the valiant Nutcracker.

And at the same moment the trumpets of Fritz's hussars began to sound, while the drums of his infantry began to beat, and the rumbling of cannon was also heard. At the same time a band of musicians was formed with fat Figaros with their guitars, Swiss peasants with their horns, and Negroes with their triangles. And all these persons, though not called upon by the Nutcracker, did not the less begin to descend from shelf to shelf, playing the beautiful march of the "British Grenadiers." The music no doubt excited the most peaceably-inclined puppets; for, at the same moment, a kind of militia, commanded by the beadle of the parish, was formed, consisting of harlequins, punches, clowns, and pantaloons. Arming themselves with anything that fell in their way, they were soon ready for battle. All was bustle, even to a man-cook, who, quitting his fire, came down with his spit, on which

was a half-roasted turkey, and went and took his place in the ranks. The Nutcracker placed himself at the head of this valiant battalion, which, to the shame of the regular troops, was ready first.

I must tell you everything, or else you might think that I am inclined to be too favourable to that glorious militia; and therefore I must say that if the infantry and cavalry of Master Fritz were not ready so soon as the others, it was because they were all shut up in four boxes. The poor prisoners might therefore well hear the trumpet and drum which called them to battle: they were shut up, and could not get out. Mary heard them stirring in their boxes, like cray-fish in a basket; but, in spite of their efforts, they could not free themselves. At length the grenadiers, less tightly fastened in than the others, succeeded in raising the lid of their box, and then helped to liberate the light infantry. In another instant, these were free; and, well knowing how useful cavalry is in a battle, they hastened to release the hussars, who began to canter gaily about, and range themselves four deep upon the flanks.

But if the regular troops were thus somewhat behindhand, in consequence of the excellent discipline in which Fritz maintained them, they speedily repaired the lost time: for infantry, cavalry, and artillery began to descend with the fury of an avalanche, amidst the plaudits of Miss Rose and Miss Clara, who clapped their hands as they passed, and encouraged them with their voices, as the ladies from whom they were descended most likely were wont to do in the days of ancient chivalry.

Meantime the king of the mice perceived that he had to encounter an entire army. In fact, the Nutcracker was in the centre of his gallant band of militia; on the left was the regiment of hussars, waiting only the moment to charge; on the right was stationed a formidable battalion of infantry; while, upon a footstool which commanded the entire scene of battle, was a park of ten cannon. In addition to these forces, a powerful reserve, composed of gingerbread men, and warriors made of sugar of different colours, had remained in the cupboard, and already began to bustle about. The king of the mice had, however, gone too far to retreat; and he gave the signal by a squeak, which was repeated by all the forces under his command.

At the same moment the battery on the footstool replied with a volley of shot amongst the masses of mice.

The regiment of hussars rushed onward to the charge, so that on one side the dust raised by their horses feet, and on the other the smoke of the cannon, concealed their plain of battle from the eyes of Mary.

But in the midst of the roar of cannon, the shouts of the combatants, and the groans of the dying, she heard the voice of the Nutcracker ever rising above the din.

"Serjeant Harlequin," he cried, "take twenty men, and fall upon the flank of the enemy. Lieutenant Punch, form into a square. Captain Puppet, fire in platoons. Colonel of Hussars, charge in masses, and not four deep, as you are doing. Bravo, good leaden soldiers—bravo! If all my troops behave as well as you, the day is ours!"

But, by these encouraging words even, Mary was at no loss to perceive that the battle was deadly, and that the victory remained doubtful. The mice, thrown back by the hussars—decimated by the fire of platoons—and shattered by the park of artillery, returned again and again to the charge, biting and tearing all who came in their way. It was like the combats in the days of chivalry—a furious struggle foot to foot and hand to hand, each one bent upon attack or defence, without waiting to think of his neighbour. Nutcracker vainly endeavoured to direct the evolutions in a disciplined manner, and form his troops into dense columns. The hussars, assailed by numerous corps of mice, were scattered, and failed to rally round their colonel; a vast battalion of enemy had cut them off from the main body of their army, and had actually advanced up to the militia, which performed prodigies of valour. The beadle of the parish used his battle-axe most gallantly; the man-cook ran whole ranks of mice through with his spit; the leaden soldiers remained firm as a wall; but Harlequin and his twenty men had been driven back, and were forced to retreat under cover of the battery; and Lieutenant Punch's square had been broken up. The remains of his troops fled and threw the militia into disorder; and Captain Puppet, doubtless for want of cartridges, had ceased to fire, and was in full retreat. In consequence of this backward movement through the line, the park of cannon was exposed. The king of the mice, perceiving that the success of the fight depended upon the capture of that battery, ordered his bravest troops to attack it. The footstool was accordingly stormed in a moment, and the artillerymen were cut to pieces by the side of their cannon. One of them set fire to his powder-waggon, and met an heroic death with twenty of his comrades. But all this display was useless against numbers; and in a short time a volley of shot, fired upon them from their own cannon, and which swept the forces commanded by the Nutcracker, convinced him that the battery of the footstool had fallen into the hands of the enemy.

From that moment the battle was lost, and the Nutcracker now thought only of beating an honourable retreat: but, in order to give breathing time to his troops, he summoned the reserve to his aid.

Thereupon, the gingerbread men and the corps of sugar warriors descended from the cupboard and took part in the battle. They were certainly fresh, but very inexperienced, troops: the gingerbread men especially were very awkward, and, hitting right and left, did as much injury to friends as to enemies. The sugar warriors stood firm; but they were of such different natures—emperors, knights, Tyrolese peasants, gardeners, cupids, monkeys, lions, and crocodiles—that they could not combine their movements, and were strong only as a mass. Their arrival, however, produced some good; for scarcely had the mice tasted the gingerbread men and the sugar warriors, when they left the leaden soldiers, whom they found very hard to bite, and turned also from the punches, harlequins, beadles, and cooks, who were only stuffed with bran, to fall upon the unfortunate reserve, which in a moment was surrounded by thousands of mice, and, after an heroic defence, devoured arms and baggage.

Nutcracker attempted to profit by that moment to rally his army; but the terrible spectacle of the destruction of the reserve had struck terror to the bravest hearts. Captain Puppet was as pale as death; Harlequin's clothes were in rags; a mouse had penetrated into Punch's hump, and, like the youthful Spartan's fox, began to devour his entrails; and not only was the colonel of the hussars a prisoner with a large portion of his troops, but the mice had even formed a squadron of cavalry, by means of horses thus taken.

The unfortunate Nutcracker had no chance of victory left: he could not even retreat with honour; and therefore he determined to die.

He placed himself at the head of a small body of men, resolved like himself to sell their lives dearly.

In the meantime terror reigned among the dolls: Miss Clara and Miss Rose wrung their hands, and gave vent to loud cries.

"Alas!" exclaimed Miss Clara; "must I die in the flower of my youth—I, the daughter of a king, and born to such brilliant destinies?"

"Alas!" said Miss Rose; "am I doomed to fall into the hands of the enemy, and be devoured by the filthy mice?"

The other dolls ran about in tears; their cries mingling with those of Miss Clara and Miss Rose. Meanwhile matters went worse and worse with Nutcracker: he was abandoned by the few friends who had remained faithful to him. The remains of the squadron of hussars took refuge in the cupboard; the leaden soldiers had all fallen into the power of the enemy; the cannoneers had long previously been dispersed; and the militia was cut to pieces, like the three hundred Spartans of Leonidas, without yielding a step. Nutcracker had planted himself against the lower part of the cupboard, which he vainly sought to climb up: he could not do so without the aid of Miss Rose or Miss Clara; and they had found nothing better to do than to faint. Nutcracker made a last effort, collected all his courage, and cried in an agony of despair, "A horse! a horse! my kingdom for a horse!" But, as in the case of Richard III, his voice remained without even an echo—or rather betrayed him to the enemy. Two of the rifle-brigade of the mice seized upon his wooden cloak; and at the same time the king of the mice cried with his seven mouths, "On your heads, take him alive! Remember that I have my mother to avenge! This punishment must serve as an example to all future Nutcrackers!"

And, with these words, the king rushed upon the prisoner.

But Mary could no longer support that horrible spectacle.

"Oh! my poor Nutcracker!" she exclaimed: "I love you with all my heart, and cannot see you die thus!"

At the same moment, by a natural impulse and without precisely knowing what she was doing, Mary took off one of her shoes, and threw it with all her force in the midst of the combatants. Her aim was so good that the shoe hit the king of the mice, and made him roll over in the dust. A moment afterwards, king and army—conquerors and conquered—all alike disappeared, as if by enchantment. Mary felt a more severe pain than before in her arm. She endeavoured to reach an arm-chair to sit down; but her strength failed her—and she fainted!

The Illness

When Mary awoke from her deep sleep, she found herself lying in her little bed, and the sun penetrated radiant and brilliant through the windows. By her side was seated a gentleman whom she shortly perceived to be a surgeon named Vandelstern, and who said in a low voice, the moment she opened her eyes, "She is awake."

Then the judge's wife advanced towards the bed, and gazed upon her daughter for a long time with an anxious air.

"Ah! my dear mamma," exclaimed little Mary, upon seeing her mother; "are all those horrible mice gone? and is my poor Nutcracker saved?"

"For the love of heaven, my dear Mary, do not repeat all that nonsense," said the lady. "What have mice, I should like to know, to do with the Nutcracker? But you, naughty girl, have frightened us all sadly. And it is always so when children are obstinate and will not obey their parents. You played with your toys very late last night: you most likely fell asleep; and it is probable that a little mouse frightened you. At all events, in your alarm, you thrust your elbow through one of the panes of the cupboard, and cut your arm in such a manner that Mr. Vandlestern, who has just extracted the fragments of glass, declares that you ran a risk of cutting an artery and dying through loss of blood. Heaven be thanked that I awoke—I know not at what o'clock—and that, recollecting how I had left you in the room, I went down to look after you. Poor child! you were stretched upon the floor, near the cupboard; and all round you were strewed the dolls, the puppets, the punches, the leaden soldiers, pieces of the gingerbread men, and Fritz's hussars—all scattered about pell-mell—while in your arms you held the Nutcracker. But how was it that you had taken off one of your shoes, and that it was at some distance from you?"

"Ah! my dear mother," said Mary, shuddering as she thought of what had taken place; "all that you saw was caused by the great battle that took place between the puppets and the mice: but the reason of my terror was

that I saw the victorious mice about to seize upon the poor Nutcracker, who commanded the puppets;—and it was then that I threw my shoe at the king of the mice. After that, I know not what happened."

The surgeon made a sign to the judge's lady, who said in a soft tone to Mary, "Do not think any more of all that, my dear child. All the mice are gone, and the little Nutcracker is safe and comfortable in the glass cupboard."

The judge then entered the room, and conversed for a long time with the surgeon; but of all that they said Mary could only catch these words—"It is delirium."

Mary saw immediately that her story was not believed, but that it was looked upon as fable; and she did not say any more upon the subject, but allowed those around her to have their own way. For she was anxious to get up as soon as possible and pay a visit to the poor Nutcracker. She, however, knew she had escaped safe and sound from the battle; and that was all she cared about for the present.

Nevertheless Mary was very restless. She could not play, on account of her wounded arm; and when she tried to read or look over her picture-books, everything swam so before her eyes that she was obliged to give up the task. The time hung very heavily upon her hands; and she looked forward with impatience to the evening, because her mamma would come and sit by her, and tell her pleasant stories.

One evening, the judge's wife had just ended the pretty tale of "Prince Facardin," when the door opened, and Godfather Drosselmayer thrust in his head, saying, "I must see with my own eyes how the little invalid gets on."

But when Mary perceived Godfather Drosselmayer with his glass wig, his black patch, and his drab frock-coat, the remembrance of the night when the Nutcracker lost the famous battle against the mice, returned so forcibly to her mind, that she could not prevent herself from crying out, "O Godpapa Drosselmayer, you were really very ugly! I saw you quite plainly, when you were astride upon the clock, and when you covered it with your wings to prevent it from striking, because it would have frightened away the mice. I heard you call the king with the seven heads. Why did you not come to the aid of my poor Nutcracker, naughty Godpapa Drosselmayer; for, by not coming, you were the cause of my hurting myself and having to keep to my bed."

The judge's wife listened to all this with a kind of stupor; for she thought that the poor little girl was relapsing into delirium. She therefore said, in a low tone of alarm,

"What are you talking about, Mary? are you taking leave of your senses?"

"Oh! no," answered Mary; "and Godpapa Drosselmayer knows that I am telling the truth."

But the godfather, without saying a word, made horrible faces, like a man who was sitting upon thorns; then all of a sudden he began to chant these lines in a gloomy sing-song tone:—

"Old clock-bell, beat
　　　Low, dull, and hoarse:—
　Advance, retreat,
　　　Thou gallant force!

"The bell's lone sound proclaims around
　　　The hour of deep mid-night;
　And the piercing note from the screech-owl's throat
　　　Puts the king himself to flight.

"Old clock-bell, beat
　　　Low, dull, and hoarse:—
　Advance, retreat,
　　　Thou gallant force!"

Mary contemplated Godfather Drosselmayer with increasing terror; for he now seemed to her more hideously ugly than usual. She would indeed have been dreadfully afraid of him, if her mother had not been present, and if Fritz had not at that moment entered the room with a loud shout of laughter.

"Do you know, Godpapa Drosselmayer," said Fritz, "that you are uncommonly amusing to-day: you seem to

move about just like my punch that stands behind the store; and, as for the song, it is not common sense."

"My dear doctor," she said, "your song is indeed very strange, and appears to me to be only calculated to make little Mary worse."

"Nonsense!" cried Godfather Drosselmayer: "do you not recognise the old chant which I am in the habit of humming when I mend your clocks?"

At the same time he seated himself near Mary's bed, and said to her in a rapid tone, "Do not be angry with me, my dear child, because I did not tear out the fourteen eyes of the king of the mice with my own hands; but I knew what I was about—and now, as I am anxious to make it up with you, I will tell you a story."

"What story?" asked Mary.

"*The History of the Crackatook Nut and Princess Pirlipata*. Do you know it?"

"No, my dear godpapa," replied Mary, whom the offer of a story reconciled to the doctor that moment. "Go on."

"My dear doctor," said the judge's wife, "I hope that your story will not be so melancholy as your song?"

"Oh, no, my dear lady," returned Godfather Drosselmayer. "On the contrary, it is very amusing."

"Tell it to us, then!" cried both the children.

Godfather Drosselmayer accordingly began in the following manner.

THE HISTORY OF THE CRACKATOOK NUT
AND PRINCESS PIRLIPATA

How Princess Pirlipata Was Born, and How the Event Produced the Greatest Joy to Her Parents

There was lately, in the neighbourhood of Nuremberg, a little kingdom, which was not Prussia, nor Poland, nor Bavaria, nor the Palatinate, and which was governed by a king.

This king's wife, who was consequently a queen, became the mother of a little girl, who was therefore a princess by birth, and received the sweet name of Pirlipata.

The king was instantly informed of the event, and he hastened out of breath to see the pretty infant in her cradle. The joy which he felt in being the father of so charming a child, carried him to such an extreme that, quite forgetting himself, he uttered loud cries of joy, and began to dance around the room, crying, "Oh! who has ever seen anything so beautiful as my Pirlapatetta?"

Then, as the king had been followed into the room by his ministers, his generals, the great officers of state, the chief judges, the councillors, and the puisne judges, they all began dancing around the room as the king, singing:

> "Great monarch, we ne'er
>   In this world did see
> A child so fair
> As the one that there
>   Has been given to thee!
>   Oh! ne'er, and Oh! ne'er,
>   Was there child so fair!"

And, indeed—although I may surprise you by saying so—there was not a word of flattery in all this; for, since the creation of the world, a sweeter child than Princess Pirlipata never has been seen. Her little face appeared to be made of the softest silken tissue, like the white rosy tints of the lily combined. Here eyes were of the purest and brightest blue; and nothing was more charming than to behold the golden thread of her hair, flowing in delicate curls over shoulders as white as alabaster. Moreover, Pirlipata, when born, was already provided with two complete rows of the most pearly teeth, with which—two hours after her birth—she bit the finger of the lord chancellor so hard, when, being near sighted, he stooped down to look close at her, that, although he belonged to the sect of stoic philosophers, he cried out according to some, "Oh! the dickens!" whereas others affirm, to the honour of philosophy, that he only said, "Oh! Oh!" However, up to the present day opinions are divided upon this important subject, neither party being willing to yield to the other. Indeed, the only point on which the *Dickensonians* and the *Ohists* are agreed is, that the princess really did bite the finger of the lord high chancellor. The country thereby learnt that there was as much spirit as beauty belonging to the charming Pirlipata.

Everyone was therefore happy in a kingdom so blest by heaven, save the queen herself, who was anxious and uneasy, no person knew why. But what chiefly struck people with surprise, was the care with which the timid mother had the cradle of the infant watched. In fact, besides having all the doors guarded by sentinels, and in addition to the two regular nurses, the queen had six other nurses to sit round the cradle, and who were relieved by a half-a-dozen others at night. But what caused the greatest interest, and which no one could understand, was that each of these six nurses was compelled to hold a cat upon her knees, and to tickle it all night so as to prevent it from sleeping, and keep it purring.

I am certain, my dear children, that you are as curious as the inhabitants of that little kingdom without a name, to know why these extra nurses were forced to hold cats upon their knees, and to tickle them in such a way that they should never cease purring; but, as you would vainly endeavour to find out the secret of that enigma, I shall explain it to you, in order to save you the headache which would not fail to be the result of your guess-work.

It happened one day that half-a-dozen great kings took it into their heads to pay a visit to the future father of Princess Pirlipata, for at that time the princess was not born. They were accompanied by the royal princes, the hereditary grand dukes, and the heirs apparent, all most agreeable personages. This arrival was the signal for the king whom they visited, and who was a most hospitable monarch, to make a large drain upon his treasury, and give tournaments, feasts, and dramatic representations. But this was not all. He having learnt from the intendant of the royal kitchen, that the astronomer royal of the court was favourable for killing pigs, and the conjunction of the stars foretold that the year would be propitious for sausage-making, the king commanded a tremendous slaughter of pigs to take place in the court-yard. Then, ordering his carriage, he went in person to call upon all the kings and princes staying in his capital, and invite them to dine with him; for he was resolved to surprise them by the splendid banquet which he intended to give them. On his return to the palace, he retired to the queen's apartment, and going to her, said in a coaxing tone, with which he was always accustomed to make her do anything he wished,

"My most particular and very dear love, you have not forgotten—have you—how doatingly fond I am of black puddings? You surely have not forgotten that?"

The queen understood by the first word what the king wanted of her. In fact she knew by his cunning address, that she must now proceed, as she had done many times before, to the very useful occupation of making, with her own royal hands, the greatest possible quantity of sausages, polonies, and black puddings. She therefore smiled at that proposal of her husband; for although filling with dignity the high situation of queen, she was less proud of the compliments paid her upon the manner in which she bore the sceptre and the crown, than of those bestowed on her skill in making a black pudding, or any other dish. She therefore contented herself by curtseying gracefully to her husband, saying that she was quite ready to make him the puddings which he required.

The grand treasurer accordingly received orders to carry the immense enamelled cauldron and the large silver saucepans to the royal kitchens, so that the queen might make the black puddings, the polonies, and the sausages. An enormous fire was made with sandal-wood; the queen put on her apron of white damask, and in a short time delicious odours steamed from the cauldron. Those sweet perfumes spread through the passages, penetrated into all the rooms, and reached the throne room where the king was holding a privy council. The king was very fond of good eating, and the smell made a profound impression upon him. Nevertheless, as he was a wise prince, and was famed for his habits of self-command, he resisted for a long time the feeling which attracted him towards the kitchens; but at last, in spite of the command

which he exercised over himself, he was compelled to yield to the inclination that now ruled him.

"My lords and gentlemen," he accordingly said, rising from his throne, "with your permission I will retire for a few moments; pray wait for me." Then this great king hastened through the passages and corridors to the kitchen, embraced his wife tenderly, stirred the contents of the cauldron with his golden sceptre, and tasted them with the tip of his tongue. Having thus calmed his mind, he returned to the council, and resumed, though somewhat abstractedly, the subject of discussion.

He had left the kitchen just at the important moment when the fat, cut up in small pieces, was about to be broiled upon the silver gridirons. The queen, encouraged by his praises, now commenced that important operation; and the first drops of grease had just dripped upon the live coals, when a squeaking voice was heard to chant the following lines:

"Dear sister, pray give to the queen of the mice,
 A piece of that fat which is grilling so nice;
 To me a good dinner is something so rare,
 That I hope of the fat you will give me a share."

The queen immediately recognised the voice that thus spoke; it was the voice of Dame Mousey.

Dame Mousey had lived for many years in the pal-ace. She declared herself to be a relation of the royal family, and was queen of the kingdom of mice. She there-fore maintained a numerous court beneath the kitchen hearth-stone.

The queen was a kind and good-natured woman; and although she would not publicly recognise Dame Mousey as a sister and a sovereign, she nevertheless showed her in private a thousand flattering attentions. Her husband, more particular than herself, had often reproached her for thus lowering herself. But on the present occasion she could not find it in her heart to refuse the request of her little friend; and she accordingly said, "Come, Dame Mousey, without fear, and taste my pork-fat as much as you like. I give you full leave to do so."

Dame Mousey accordingly leapt upon the hearth, quite gay and happy, and took with her little paws the pieces of fat which the queen gave her.

But, behold! the murmurs of joy which escaped the mouth of Dame Mousey, and the delicious smell of the morsels of fat on the gridiron, reached her seven sons, then her relations, and next her friends, all of whom were terribly addicted to gourmandizing, and who now fell upon the fat with such fury, that the queen was obliged, hospitable as she was, to remind them that if they contin-ued at that rate only five minutes more, there would not be enough fat left for the black puddings. But, in spite of the justice of this remonstrance, the seven sons of Dame Mousey took no heed of them; and setting a bad example to their relations and friends, rushed upon their aunt's fat, which would have entirely disappeared, had not the cries of the queen brought the man-cook and scullery boys, all armed with brushes and brooms, to drive the mice back again under the hearth-stone. But the victory, although complete, came somewhat too late; for there scarcely remained a quarter enough fat necessary for the polonies, the sausages, and the black puddings. The remnant, however, was scientifically divided by the royal mathematician, who was sent for in all possible haste, between the large cauldron containing the materials for the puddings, and the two saucepans in which the sausages and polonies were cooking.

Half an hour after this event, the cannon fired, the clarions and trumpets sounded, and then came the potentates, the royal princes, the hereditary dukes, and the heirs apparent to the thrones, all dressed in their most splendid clothes, and some riding on gallant chargers. The king received them on the threshold of the palace, in the most courteous manner possible; then, having conducted them to the banqueting room, he took his seat at the head of the table in his quality of sovereignhood, and

having the crown upon his head and the sceptre in his hand. The guests all placed themselves at table according to their rank, as crowned kings, royal princes, hereditary dukes, or heirs apparent.

The board was covered with dainties, and everything went well during the soup and the first course. But when the polonies were placed on the table, the king seemed to be agitated; when the sausages were served up, he grew very pale; and when the black puddings were brought in, he raised his eyes to heaven, sighs escaped his breast, and a terrible grief seemed to rend his soul. At length he fell back in his chair, and covered his face with his hands, sobbing and moaning in so lamentable a manner, that all the guests rose from their seats and surrounded him with great anxiety. At length the crisis seemed very serious; the court physician could not feel the beating of the pulse of the unfortunate monarch, who was thus overwhelmed with the weight of the most profound, the most frightful, and the most unheard of calamity. At length, upon the most violent remedies, such as burnt feathers, volatile salts, and cold keys thrust down the back, had been employed, the king seemed to return to himself. He opened his eyes, and said in a scarcely audible tone, "*not enough fat!*"

At these words, the queen grew pale in her turn, she threw herself at his feet, crying in a voice interrupted by sobs, "Oh! my unfortunate, unhappy, and royal husband, What grief have I not caused you, by refusing to listen to the advice which you have so often given me! But you behold the guilty one at your feet, and you can punish her as severely as you think fit."

"What is the matter?" demanded the king, "and what has happened that I know not of?"

"Alas! alas!" answered the queen, to whom her husband had never spoken in so cross a tone; "Alas! Dame Mousey, her seven sons, her nephews, her cousins, and her friends, devoured the fat."

But the queen could not say any more; her strength failed her, she fell back and fainted.

Then the king rose in a great rage, and cried in a terrible voice, "Let her ladyship the royal housekeeper explain what all this means! Come, speak!"

Then the royal housekeeper related all that she knew; namely, that being alarmed by the queen's cries, she ran and beheld the majesty beset by the entire family of Dame Mousey, and that, having summoned the cooks and scullery boys, the plunderers were compelled to retreat.

The king, perceiving that this was a case of high treason, resumed all his dignity and calmness, and commanded the privy council to meet that minute, the matter being of the utmost importance. The council assembled, the business was explained, and it was decided by a majority of voices, "That Dame Mousey, being accused of having eaten the fat destined for the sausages, the polonies, and the black puddings of the king, should be tried for the same offence; and that if the said Dame Mousey was found guilty, she and all her race should be banished from the kingdom, and all her good or possessions, namely, lands, castles, palaces, and royal residencies should be confiscated."

Then the king observed to his councillors that while the trial lasted, Dame Mousey and her family would have sufficient time to devour all the fat in the royal kitchens, which would expose him to the same privation as that which he had just endured in the presence of six crowned heads, without reckoning royal princes, hereditary dukes, and heirs apparent. He therefore demanded a discretionary power in respect to dame Mousey and her family.

The privy council divided, for the form of the thing, but the discretionary power was voted, as you may well suppose, by a large majority.

Then the king sent one of his best carriages, preceded by a courier that greater speed might be used, to a very

skilful mechanic who lived at Nuremberg, and whose name was Christian Elias Drosselmayer. This mechanic was requested to proceed that moment to the palace upon urgent business. Christian Elias Drosselmayer immediately obeyed, for he felt convinced that the king required him to make some work of art. Stepping into the vehicle, he travelled day and night, until he arrived in the king's presence. Indeed, such was his haste, that he had not waited to change the drab-coloured coat which he usually wore. But instead of being angry at that breach of etiquette, the king was much pleased with his haste; for if the famous mechanic had committed a fault, it was in his anxiety to obey the kings commands.

The king took Christian Elias Drosselmayer into his private chamber, and explained to him the position of affairs; namely, that it was decided upon to make a striking example of the race of mice throughout the kingdom; that attracted by the fame of his skill, the king had fixed upon him to put the decree of justice into execution; and that the said king's only fear was lest the mechanic, skilful though he were, should perceive insurmountable difficulties in the way of appeasing the royal anger.

But Christian Elias Drosselmayer reassured the king, promising that in eight days there should not be a single mouse left in the kingdom.

In a word, that very same day he set to work to make several ingenious little oblong boxes, inside which he placed a morsel of fat at the end of a piece of wire. By seizing upon the fat, the plunderer, whoever he might be, caused the door to shut down behind him, and thus became a prisoner. In less than a week, a hundred of these boxes were made, and placed, not only beneath the hearth-stone, but in all the garrets, lofts, and cellars of the palace. Dame Mousey was far too cunning and sagacious not to discover at the first glance the stratagem of Master Drosselmayer. She therefore assembled her seven sons, their nephews, and their cousins, to warn them of the snare that was laid for them. But, after having appeared to listen to her, and the veneration which her years commanded, they withdrew, laughing at her terrors; then, attracted by the smell of the fried pork-fat, they resolved, in spite of the representations made to them, to profit by the charity that came they knew not whence.

At the expiration of twenty-four hours, the seven sons of Dame Mousey, eighteen of her nephews, fifty of her cousins, and two hundred and thirty-five of her other connexions, without reckoning thousands of her subjects, were caught in the mouse-traps and ignominiously executed.

Then did Dame Mousey, with the remnant of her court and the rest of her subjects, resolve upon abandoning a place covered with the blood of her massacred relatives and friends. The tidings of that resolution became known and reached the ears of the king. His majesty expressed his satisfaction, and the poets of the court

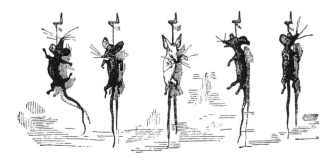

composed sonnets upon his victory, while the courtiers compared him to Sesostris, Alexander, and Cæsar.

The queen was alone anxious and uneasy; she knew Dame Mousey well, and suspected that she would not leave unavenged the death of her relations and friends. And, in fact, at the very moment when the queen, by way of atoning for her previous fault, was preparing with her own hands a liver soup for the king, who doated upon that dish, Dame Mousey suddenly appeared and chanted the following lines:

"Thine husband, void of pity and of fear,
  Hath slain my cousins, sons, and nephews dear;
    But list, O queen! to the decrees of fate:
  The child which heaven will shortly give to thee,
  And which the object of thy love will be,
    Shall bear the rage of my vindictive hate.

"Thine husband owneth castles, cannons, towers,
  A council's wisdom, and an army's powers,
    Mechanics, ministers, mouse-traps, and snares:
  None of all these, alas! to me belong;
  But heaven hath given me teeth, sharp, firm, and
  strong,
    That I may rend in pieces royal heirs."

Having sung these words she disappeared, and no one saw her afterwards. But the queen, who expected a little baby, was so overcome by the prophecy, that she upset the liver soup into the fire.

Thus, for the second time, was Dame Mousey the cause of depriving the king of one of his favourite dishes,

whereat he fell into a dreadful rage. He, however, rejoiced more than ever at the step he had taken to ride his country of the mice.

It is scarcely necessary to say that Christian Edward Drosselmayer was sent away well rewarded, and returned in triumph to Nuremberg.

How, in Spite of the Precautions Taken by the Queen, Dame Mousey Accomplishes Her Threat in Regard to Princess Pirlipata

And now, my dear children, you know as well as I do, wherefore the queen had Princess Pirlipata watched with such wonderful care. She feared the vengeance of Dame Mousey; for, according to what Dame Mousey had said, there could be nothing less in store for the heiress of this little kingdom without a name, than the loss of her life, or at all events her beauty; which last affliction is considered by some people worse for one of her sex. What redoubled the fears of the queen was, that the machines invented by Master Drosselmayer were totally useless against the experience of Dame Mousey. The astronomer of the court, who was also grand prophet and grand astrologer, was fearful lest his office should be suppressed unless he gave his opinion at this important juncture: he accordingly declared that he read in the stars the great fact that the illustrious family of the cat Murr was alone capable of defending the cradle against the approach of Dame Mousey. It was for this reason that each of his six nurses was forced to hold a cat constantly upon her knees. Those cats might be considered as under-officers attached to the court; and the nurses sought to lighten the cares of the duty performed by the cats, by gently rubbing them with their fair hands.

You know, my dear children, that there are certain times when a person watches even while actually dozing; and so it was that, one evening, in spite of all the efforts which the six nurses made to the contrary, as they sat

round the cradle of the princess with the cats upon their knees, they felt sleep rapidly gaining upon them. Now, as each nurse kept her own ideas to herself, and was afraid of revealing them to their companions, hoping all the time that their drowsiness would not be perceived by others, the result was, that, one after another, they closed their eyes—their hands stopped from stroking the cats—and the cats themselves, being no longer rubbed and scratched, profited by circumstance to take a nap.

I cannot say how long this strange slumber had lasted, when, towards midnight, one of the nurses awoke with a start. All the others were in a state of profound lethargy: not a sound—not even their very breathing, was heard: the silence of death reigned around, broken only by the slight creak of the worm biting the wood. But how frightened was the nurse when she beheld a large and horrible mouse standing up near her on its hind legs, and, having plunged its head into the cradle, seemed very busy in biting the face of the princess! She rose with a cry of alarm; and at that exclamation, all the other nurses jumped up. But Dame Mousey—for she indeed it was—sprang towards one corner of the room. The cats leapt after her: alas! it was too late—Dame Mousey had disappeared by a crevice in the floor. At the same moment Princess Pirlipata, who was awoke by all that din, began to cry. Those sounds made the nurses leap with joy. "Thank God!" they said; "since Princess Pirlipata cries she is not dead!" They then all ran towards the cradle—but their despair was great indeed when they saw what had happened to that delicate and charming creature!

In fact, instead of that face of softly blended white and red—that little head, with its golden hair—those mild blue eyes, azure as the sky itself—instead of all these charms the nurses beheld an enormous and mis-shapen head upon a deformed and ugly body. Her two sweet eyes had lost their heavenly hue, and became goggle, fixed, and haggard. Her little mouth had grown from ear to ear; and her chin was covered with a beard like grizzly cotton. All this would have suited old Punch; but seemed very horrible for a young princess.

At that moment the queen entered. The twelve nurses threw themselves with their faces against the ground; while the six cats walked about to discover if there were not some open window by which they might escape upon the tiles. At the sight of her child the despair of the poor mother was something frightful to behold; and she was carried off in a fainting fit into the royal chamber. But it was chiefly the unhappy father whose sorrow was the

most desperate and painful to witness. The courtiers were compelled to put padlocks upon the windows, for fear he should throw himself out; and they were also forced to line the walls with mattresses, lest he should dash out his brains against them. His sword was of course taken away from him; and neither knife nor fork, nor any sharp or pointed instruments were left in his way. This was the more easily effected; inasmuch as he ate nothing for the two or three following days, crying without ceasing, "Oh! miserable king that I am! Oh! cruel destiny that thou art!"

Perhaps, instead of accusing destiny, the king should have remembered that, as is generally the case with mankind, he was the author of his own misfortunes; for had he known how to content himself with black pudding containing a little less fat than usual, and had he abandoned his ideas of vengeance, and left dame Mousey and her family in peace beneath the hearth-stone, the affliction which he deplored would not have happened. But we must confess that the ideas of the royal father of Princess Pirlipata did not tend at all in that direction.

On the contrary—believing, as all great men do, that they must necessarily attribute their misfortunes to others—he threw all the blame upon the skilful mechanic Christian Elias Drosselmayer. Well convinced, moreover, that if he invited him back to court to be hung or beheaded, he would not accept the invitation, he desired him to come in order to receive a new order of knighthood which had just been created for men of letters, artists, and mechanics. Master Drosselmayer was not exempt from human pride: he thought that a star would look well upon the breast of his drab surtout coat; and accordingly set off for the king's court. But his joy was soon changed into

fear; for on the frontiers of the kingdom, guards awaited him. They seized upon him, and conducted him from station to station, until they reached the capital.

The king, who was afraid of being won over to mercy, would not see Master Drosselmayer when the latter arrived at the palace; but he ordered him to be immediately conducted to the cradle of Pirlipata, with the assurance that if the princess were not restored by that day month to her former state of beauty, he would have the mechanic's head cut off.

Master Drosselmayer did not pretend to be bolder than his fellow-men, and had always hoped to die a natural death. He was therefore much frightened at this threat. Nevertheless, trusting a great deal to his knowledge, which his own modesty had never prevented him being aware of to its full extent, he acquired courage. Then he set to work to discover whether the evil would yield to any remedy, or whether it were really incurable, as he had from the first believed it to be.

With this object in view, he skilfully took off the head of the Princess, and next all her limbs. He likewise dissected the hands and feet, in order to examine, with more accuracy, not only the joints and the muscles, but also the internal formation. But, alas! the more he worked into the frame of Pirlipata, the more firmly did he become convinced that as the princess grew, the uglier she would become. He therefore joined Pirlipata together again; and then, seating himself by the side of her cradle, which he was not to quit until she had resumed her former beauty, he gave way to his melancholy thoughts.

The fourth week had already commenced, and Wednesday made its appearance, when, according to custom, the king came in to see if any change had taken place in the exterior of the princess. But when he saw that it was just the same, he shook his scepter at the mechanic, crying, "Christian Elias Drosselmayer, take care of yourself! you have only three days left to restore me my daughter just as she was wont to be; and if you remain obstinate in refusing to cure her, on Monday next you shall be beheaded."

Master Drosselmayer, who could not cure the princess, not through any obstinacy on his part, but through

actual ignorance how to do it, began to weep bitterly, surveying, with tearful eyes, Princess Pirlipata, who was cracking nuts as comfortably as if she were the most beautiful child upon the earth. Then as he beheld that melting spectacle, the mechanic was struck for the first time by that particular taste for nuts which the princess had shown since her birth; and he remembered also the singular fact that she was born with teeth. In fact, immediately after her change from beauty to ugliness she had begun to cry bitterly, until she found a nut near her: she had then cracked it, eaten the kernel, and turned around to sleep quietly. From that moment the nurses had taken good care to fill their pockets with nuts, and give her one or more whenever she made a face.

"Oh! instinct of nature! Eternal and mysterious sympathy of all created beings!" cried Christian Elias Drosselmayer, "thou showest me the door which leads to the discovery of thy secrets! I will knock at it, and it will open!"

At these words, which surprised the king, the mechanic turned towards his majesty and requested the favour of being conducted into the presence of the astronomer of the court. The king consented, but on condition that it should be with a guard. Master Drosselmayer would perhaps have been better pleased to take that little walk all alone; but, as under the circumstances he could not help himself, he was obliged to submit to what he could not prevent, and processed through the streets of the capital escorted like a felon.

On reaching the house of the astrologer, Master Drosselmayer threw himself into his arms; and they embraced each other amidst torrents of tears, for they were acquaintances of long standing, and were much attached to each other. They then retired to a private room, and examined a great number of books which treated upon likings and dislikings, and a host of other matters not a whit less profound. At length night came; and the astrologer ascending to his tower, and aided by Master Drosselmayer, who was himself very skilful in such matters, discovered, in spite of the difficulty of the heavenly circles which crossed each other in all directions, that in order to break the spell which rendered Princess Pirlipata hideous, and to restore her former beauty, she must eat the kernel of the Crackatook nut, the shell of which was so hard that the wheel of a forty-eight pounder might pass over it without breaking it. Moreover, it was necessary that this nut should be cracked in the presence of the princess, and by a young man who had never been shaved, and who had always worn boots. Lastly, it was requisite that he should present the nut to the princess, with his eyes closed, and in the same way step seven paces backward without stumbling. Such was the answer of the stars.

Drosselmayer and the astronomer had worked without ceasing for four days and four nights, to clear up this mysterious affair. It was on the Sunday evening—the king had finished his dinner, and was just beginning on the dessert—when the mechanic, who was to be beheaded the next day, entered the royal dining room, full of joy, and announced that he had discovered the means of restoring Princess Pirlipata to her beauty. At these news, the king caught him in his arms, with the most touching kindness, and asked him what those means were.

The mechanic thereupon explained to the king the result of his consultation with the astrologer.

"I knew perfectly well, Master Drosselmayer," said the king, "that all your delay was only through obstinacy. It is, however, settled at last; and after dinner we will set to work. Take care, then, dearest mechanic, to have the young man who has never been shaved, and who wears boots, in readiness in ten minutes, together with the nut Crackatook. Let him, moreover, abstain from drinking wine for the next hour, for fear he should stumble while walking backwards like a crab; but when once it is all over, tell him that he is welcome to my whole cellar, and may get as tipsy as he chooses."

But, to the great astonishment of the king, Master Drosselmayer seemed quite frightened at these words; and, as he held his tongue, the king insisted upon knowing why he remained silent and motionless instead of hastening to execute the orders of his sovereign.

"Sire," replied the mechanician, throwing himself on his knees before the king, "it is perfectly true that we have found the means of curing Princess Pirlipata, and that those means consist of her eating a Crackatook nut when it shall have been cracked by a young man who has never been shaved, and who has always worn boots; but we have not as yet either the young man or the nut—we know not where to find them, and in all probability we shall have the greatest difficulty in discovering both the nut and the Nutcracker."

At these words, the king brandished his sceptre above the head of the mechanician, crying, "Then hasten to the scaffold!"

But the queen, on her side, hastened to kneel by the side of Master Drosselmayer, and begged her august husband to remember that by cutting off the head of the mechanician he would be losing even that ray of hope which remained to them during his lifetime; that the chances were that he who had discovered the horoscope would also find the nut and the Nutcracker; that they ought to believe more firmly in the present prediction of the astronomer, inasmuch as nothing which he had hitherto prophesied

had ever come to pass, but that it was evident his presages must be fulfilled some day or another; inasmuch as the king had named him his grand prophet; and that, as the princess was not yet of an age to marry (she being now only three months old), and would not even be marriageable until she was fifteen, there was consequently a period of fourteen years and nine months during which Master Drosselmayer and the astrologer might search after the Crackatook nut and the young man who was to break it. The queen therefore suggested that a reprieve might be awarded to Christian Elias Drosselmayer, at the expiration of which he should return to surrender himself into the king's power, whether he had found the means of curing the princess, or not; and either to be generously rewarded, or put to death without mercy.

The king, who was a very just man, and who on that day especially had dined splendidly upon his two favourite dishes—namely, liver soup and black puddings—lent a favourable ear to the prayer of his wise and courageous queen. He therefore decided that the astrologer and the mechanician should that moment set out in search of the nut and the Nutcracker; for which purpose he granted fourteen years and nine months, with the condition that they should return, at the expiration of that reprieve, to place themselves in his power, so that, if they were empty-handed, he might deal with them according to his own royal pleasure.

If, on the contrary, they should make their re-appearance with the Crackatook nut which was to restore the princess to all her former beauty, the astrologer would be rewarded with a yearly pension of six hundred pounds and a telescope of honour; and the mechanician would receive a sword set with diamonds, the Order of the Golden Spider (the grand order of the state), and new frock-coat.

As for the young man who was to crack the nut, the king had no doubt of being able to find one suitable for the purpose, by means of advertisements constantly inserted in the national and foreign newspapers.

Touched by this declaration on the part of the king, which relieved them from half the difficulty of their task, Christian Elias Drosselmayer pledged his honour that he would either find the Crackatook nut, or return, like another Regulus, to place himself in the hands of the king.

That same evening the astrologer and the mechanician departed from the capital of the kingdom to commence their researches.

* * * * *

How the Mechanician and the Astrologer
Wander Over the Four Quarters of the World,
and Discover a Fifth, Without Finding
the Crackatook Nut

It was now fourteen years and five months since the astrologer and the mechanician first set out on their wanderings through all parts, without discovering a vestige of what they sought. They had first of all travelled through Europe; then they visited America, next Africa, and afterwards Asia: they even discovered a fifth part of the world, which learned men have since called New Holland, because it was discovered by two Germans! But throughout that long series of travels, although they had seen many nuts of different shapes and sizes, they never fell in with the Crackatook nut. They had, however, in alas! a vain hope, passed several years at the court of the King of Dates and at that of the Prince of Almonds: they had uselessly consulted the celebrated Academy of Grau Monkeys and the famous Naturalist Society of Squirrels; until at length they arrived, sinking with fatigue, upon the borders of the great forest which touches the feet of the Himalayan Mountains. And now they dolefully said to each other that they had only a hundred and twenty-two days to find what they sought, after a useless search of fourteen years and five months.

If I were to tell you, my dear children, the strange adventures which happened to the two travellers during that long wandering, I should occupy you every evening for an entire month, and should then weary you in the long run. I will therefore only tell you that Christian Elias Drosselmayer, who was the most eager in search after the nut,—since his head depended upon finding it,—gave himself up to greater dangers than his companion, and lost all his hair by a stroke of the sun received in the tropics. He also lost his right eye by an arrow which a Caribbean Chief aimed at him. Moreover, his drab frock-coat, which was not new when he left Germany, had literally fallen into rags and tatters. His situation was  therefore most deplorable; and yet, so much do men cling to life, that, damaged as he was by the various accidents which had befallen him, he beheld with increasing terror the approach of the moment when he must return to place himself in the power of the king.

Nevertheless, the mechanician was a man of honour: he would not break a promise so sacred as that which he had made. He accordingly resolved, whatever might happen, to set out the very next morning on his return to Germany. And indeed there was no time to lose; fourteen years

and five months had passed away, and the two travellers had only a hundred and twenty-two days, as we have already said, to reach the capital of Princess Pirlipata's father.

Christian Elias Drosselmayer accordingly made known his noble intention to his friend the astrologer; and both decided that they would set out on their return the next morning.

And, true to this intention, the travellers resumed their journey at daybreak, taking the direction of Bagdad. From Bagdad they proceeded to Alexandria, where they embarked for Venice. From Venice they passed through the Tyrol; and from the Tyrol they entered into the kingdom of Pirlipata's father, both sincerely hoping that he was either dead or in his dotage.

But, alas! it was no such thing! Upon reaching the capital, the unfortunate mechanician learnt that the worthy monarch not only had not lost his intellectual faculties, but was also in better health than ever. There was consequently no chance for him—unless Princess Pirlipata had become cured of her ugliness without any remedy at all, which was not possible; or, that the king's heart had softened, which was not probable—of escaping the dreadful fate which threatened him.

He did not however present himself the less boldly at the gate of the palace, for he was sustained by the idea that he was doing an heroic action; and he accordingly desired to speak to the king.

The king, who was of easy access, and who gave an audience to whomsoever he had business with, ordered the grand master of the ceremonies to bring the strangers into his presence.

The grand master of the ceremonies then stated that the strangers were of a most villainous appearance, and could not possibly be worse dressed. But the king answered that it was wrong to judge the heart by the countenance, and the gown did not make the parson.

Thereupon, the grand master of the ceremonies, having perceived the correctness of these observations, bowed respectfully and proceeded to fetch the mechanician and the astrologer.

The king was the same as ever, and they immediately recognised him; but the travellers were so changed, especially poor Elias Drosselmayer, that they were obliged to declare who they were.

Upon seeing the two travellers return of their own accord, the king gave a sign of joy, for he felt convinced that they would not have come back if they had not found the Crackatook nut. But he was speedily undeceived; and the mechanician, throwing himself at his feet, confessed that, in spite of the most earnest and constant search, his friend and himself had returned empty-handed.

The king, as we have said, although of a passionate disposition, was an excellent man at bottom; he was touched by the punctuality with which Christian Elias

Drosselmayer had kept his word; and he changed the sentence of death, long before pronounced against him, into imprisonment for life. As for the astrologer, he contented himself by banishing that great sage.

But as three days were still remaining of the period of fourteen years and nine months' delay, granted by the king, Master Drosselmayer, who was deeply attached to his country, implored the king's permission to profit by those three days to visit Nuremberg once more.

This request seemed so just to the king, that he granted it without any restriction.

Master Drosselmayer, having only three days left, resolved to profit by that time as much as possible; and, having fortunately found that two places in the mail were not taken, he secured them that moment.

Now, as the astrologer was himself condemned to banishment, and as it was all the same to him which way he went, he took his departure with the mechanician.

Next morning, at about ten o'clock, they were at Nuremberg. As Master Drosselmayer had only one relation in the world, namely his brother, Christopher Zacharias Drosselmayer, who kept one of the principal toy-shops in Nuremberg, it was at his house that he alighted.

Christopher Zacharias Drosselmayer was overjoyed to see his poor brother Christian Elias, whom he had believed to be dead. In the first instance he would not admit that the man with the bald head and the black patch upon the eye was in reality his brother; but the mechanician showed him his famous drab surtout coat, which, all tattered as it was, had retained in certain parts some traces of its original colour; and in support of that first proof he mentioned so many family secrets, unknown to all save Zacharias and himself, that the toy-merchant was compelled to yield to the evidence brought forward.

He then inquired of him what had kept him so long absent from his native city, and in what country he had left his hair, his eye, and the missing pieces of his coat.

Christian Elias Drosselmayer had no motive to keep secret from his brother the events which had occurred. He began by introducing his companion in misfortune; and, this formal usage having been performed, he related his adventures from A to Z, ending them by saying that he had only a few hours to stay with his brother, because, not having found the Crackatook nut, he was on the point of being shut up in a dungeon forever.

While Christian Elias was telling his story, Christopher Zacharias had more than once twiddled his finger and thumb, turned round upon one leg, and made a certain knowing noise with his tongue. Under any other circumstances, the mechanician would have demanded of him what those signs meant; but he was so full of thought, that he saw nothing; and it was only when his brother exclaimed, "Hem! Hem!" twice, and "Oh! oh! oh!" three times, that he asked the reason of those expressions.

"The reason is," said Christopher Zacharias, "that it would be strange indeed if—but, no—and yet—"

"What do you mean?" cried the mechanician.

"If—" continued the toy-merchant.

"If what?" again said Master Drosselmayer.

But instead of giving any answer, Christopher Zacharias, who, during those short questions and answers, had no doubt collected his thoughts, threw his wig up into the air, and began to caper about, crying, "Brother, you are saved! You shall not go to prison; for either I am much mistaken, or I myself am in possession of the Crackatook nut."

And, without giving any further explanation to his astonished brother, Christopher Zacharias rushed out of the room, but returned in a moment with a box containing a large gilt filbert, which he presented to the mechanician.

The mechanician, who dared not believe in such good luck, took the nut with hesitation, and turned it round in all directions so as to examine it with the attention which it deserved. He then declared that he was of the same opinion as his brother, and that he should be much astonished if that filbert were not indeed the Crackatook nut. Thus saying, he handed it to the astrologer, and asked his opinion.

The astrologer examined it with as much attention as Master Drosselmayer had done; but shaking his head, he replied, "I should also be of the same opinion as yourself and brother, if the nut were not gilt; but I have not seen anything in the stars showing that the nut we are in search of ought to be so ornamented. Besides, how came your brother by the Crackatook nut?"

"I will explain the whole thing to you," said Christopher, "and tell you how the nut fell into my hands,

and how it came to have gilding which prevents you from recognising it, and which indeed is not its own naturally."

Then—having made them sit down, for he very wisely thought that after travelling for fourteen years and nine months they must be tired—he began as follows:

"The very day on which the king sent for you under pretence of giving you an Order of Knighthood, a stranger arrived at Nuremberg, carrying with him a bag of nuts which he had to sell. But the nut merchants of this town, being anxious to keep the monopoly themselves, quarrelled with him just opposite my shop. The stranger, with a view to defend himself more easily, placed his bag of nuts upon the ground, and the fight continued, to the great delight of the little boys and the ticket-porters; when a waggon, heavily laden, passed over the bag of nuts. Upon seeing this accident, which they attributed to the justice of heaven, the merchants considered that they were sufficiently avenged, and left the stranger alone. He picked up his bag, and all his nuts were found to be cracked, save ONE—one only—which he handed to me with a strange kind of smile requesting me to buy it for a new zwanziger of the year 1720, and declaring that the day would come when I should not repent the bargain, dear as it might seem. I felt in my pocket, and was much surprised to find a zwanziger of the kind mentioned by this man. The coincidence seemed so strange, that I gave him my zwanziger; he handed me the nut, and I took his departure.

"I placed the nut in my window for sale; and although I only asked two kreutzers more than the money I had given for it, it remained in the window for seven or eight years without finding a purchaser. I then had it gilt to increase its value; but for that purpose I uselessly spent two zwanzigers more; for the nut has been here ever since the day I bought it."

At that moment the astrologer, in whose hands the nut had remained, uttered a cry of joy. While Master Drosselmayer was listening to his brother's story, the astrologer had delicately scraped off some of the gilding of the nut; and on the shell he had found the word "Crackatook" engraven in Chinese characters.

All doubts were now cleared up; and the three individuals danced for joy, the real Crackatook nut being actually in their possession.

How, After Having Found the Crackatook Nut, the Mechanician and the Astrologer Find the Young Man Who Is to Crack It

Christian Elias Drosselmayer was in such a hurry to announce the good news to the king, that he was anxious to return by the mail that very moment; but Christian Zacharias begged him to stay at least until his son should come in. The mechanician yielded the more easily to this request, because he had not seen his nephew for fifteen years, and because, on recalling the idea of the past, he remembered that at the time when he quitted Nuremberg, he had left the said nephew a fine fat romping fellow of only three and a half, but of whom he (the uncle) was dotingly fond.

While he was thinking of these things, a handsome young man of between eighteen and nineteen entered the shop of Christopher Zacharias, whom he saluted by the name of "Father." Then Christopher Zacharias, having embraced him, presented him to Christian Elias, saying to the young man, "And now embrace your uncle."

The young man hesitated; for Uncle Drosselmayer, with his frock-coat in rags, his bald head, and the plaster upon his eye, did not seem a very inviting person. But his father observed the hesitation, and as he was fearful that Christian Elias's feelings would be wounded, he pushed his son forward, and thrust him into the arms of the mechanician.

In the meantime the astrologer had kept his eyes fixed upon the young man with a steady attention which seemed so singular that the youth felt ill at his ease in being so stared at, and left the room.

The astrologer then put several questions to Christopher Zacharias concerning his son; and the father answered them with all the enthusiasm of a fond parent.

Young Drosselmayer was, as his appearance indicated, between seventeen and eighteen. From his earliest years he had been so funny and yet so tractable, that his mother had taken a delight in dressing him like some of the puppets which her husband sold: namely, sometimes as a student, sometimes as a postilion, sometimes as a Hungarian, but always in a garb that required boots; because, as he possessed the prettiest little foot in the world, but had a rather small calf, the boots showed off the little foot, and concealed the fault of the calf.

"And so," said the astrologer to Christopher Zacharias, "your son has always worn boots?"

Christian Elias now stared in his turn.

"My son has never worn anything but boots," replied the toy-man. "At the age of ten," he continued, "I sent him to the university of Tubingen, where he remained till he was eighteen, without contracting any of the bad hab-

its of his companions, such as drinking, swearing, and fighting. The only weakness of which I believe him to be guilty, is that he allows the four or five wretched hairs which he has upon his chin to grow, without permitting a barber to touch his countenance.

"And thus," said the astrologer, "your son has never been shaved?"

Christian Elias stared more and more.

"Never," answered Christopher Zacharias.

"And during the holidays," continued the astrologer, "how did he pass his time?"

"Why," replied the father, "he used to remain in the shop, in his becoming student's dress; and, through pure good-nature, he cracked nuts for all the young ladies who came to the shop to buy toys and who, on that account, called him *Nutcracker.*"

"Nutcracker!" cried the mechanician.

"Nutcracker!" repeated the astrologer in his turn.

And then they looked at each other while Christopher Zacharias looked at them both.

"My dear sir," said the astrologer to the toy-man, "in my opinion your fortune is as good as made."

The toy-man, who had not heard this prophecy without a feeling of pleasure, required an explanation, which the astrologer, however, put off until the next morning.

When the mechanician and the astrologer were shown to their apartment, and were alone together, the astrologer embraced his friend, crying, "It is he! We have him!"

"Do you think so?" demanded Christian Elias, in the tone of a man who had his doubts, but who only wished to be convinced.

"Can there be any uncertainty?" exclaimed the astrologer: "he has all the necessary qualifications!"

"Let us sum them up."

"He has never worn anything but boots."

"True!"

"He has never been shaved."

"True, again!"

"And through good-nature, he has stood in his father's shop to crack nuts for young persons, who never called him by any other name than *Nutcracker*."

"All this is quite true."

"My dear friend," added the astrologer, "one stroke of good luck never comes alone. But if you still doubt, let us go and consult the stars."

They accordingly ascended to the roof of the house; and, having drawn the young man's horoscope, discovered that he was intended for great things.

This prophecy, which confirmed all the astrologer's hopes, forced the mechanician to adopt his opinion.

"And now," said the astrologer, in a triumphant tone, "there are only two things which we must not neglect."

"What are they?" demanded Christian Elias.

"The first, is that you must fit to the nape of your nephew's neck a large piece of wood, which must be so well connected to the lower jaw that it will increase its power by the fact of pressure."

"Nothing is more easy," answered Christian Elias; "it is the A, B, C of mechanics."

"The second thing," continued the astrologer, "is, that on arriving at the residence of the king, we must carefully conceal the fact that we have brought with us the young

man who is destined to crack the Crackatook nut. For my opinion is that the more teeth there are broken, and the more jaws there are dislocated in trying to break the Crackatook nut,

the more eager the king will be to offer a great reward to him who shall succeed where so many have failed."

"My dear friend," answered the mechanician, "you are a man of sound sense. Let us go to bed."

And, with these words, having quitted the top of the house, they descended to their bed-room, where, having drawn their cotton night-caps over their ears, they slept more comfortably than they had done for fourteen years and nine months past.

On the following morning, at an early hour, the two friends went down to the apartment of Christopher Zacharias, and told him all the fine plans they had formed the evening before. Now, as the toy-man was not wanting in ambition, and as, in his paternal fondness, he fancied that his son must certainly possess the strongest jaws in all Germany, he gladly assented to the arrangement, which was to take from his shop not only the nut but also the *Nutcracker*.

The young man himself was more difficult to persuade. The wooden counter-balance which it was proposed to fix to the back of his neck, instead of the pretty little tie which kept his hair in such neat folds, particularly vexed him. But his father, his uncle, and the astrologer made him such splendid promises, that he consented. Christian Elias Drosselmayer, therefore, went to work that moment; the wooden balance was soon made; and it was strongly fixed to the nape of the young man now so full of hope. Let me also state, to satisfy your curiosity, that the contrivance worked so well that on the very first the skilful mechanician received brilliant proofs of his success, for the young man was enabled to crack the hardest apricot-stones, and the most obstinate peach-stones.

These trials having been made, the astrologer, the mechanician, and young Drosselmayer set out immediately for the king's dwellings. Christopher Zacharias was anxious to go with them; but, as he was forced to take care of his shop, that excellent father resigned himself to necessity, and remained behind at Nuremberg.

End of the History of Princess Pirlipata

The mechanician, on reaching the capital, took good care to leave young Drosselmayer at the inn where they put up. They then proceeded to the palace to announce that having vainly sought the Crackatook nut all over the world, they had at length found it at Nuremberg. But of him who was to crack it, they said not a word, according to the arrangement made between them.

The joy at the palace was very great. The king sent directly for the privy councillor who had the care of the public mind, and who acted as censor in respect to the newspapers; and this great man, by the king's command,

drew up an article to be inserted in the *Royal Gazette*, and which all other newspapers were ordered to copy, to the effect that "*all persons who fancied that they had teeth good enough to break the Crackatook nut, were to present themselves at the palace, and if they succeeded, would be liberally rewarded for their trouble.*"

This circumstance was well-suited to show how rich the kingdom was in strong jaws. The candidates were so numerous, that the king was forced to form a jury, the foreman of whom was the crown dentist; and their duty was to examine all the competitors, to see if they had all their thirty-two teeth perfect, and whether any were decayed.

Three thousand five hundred candidates were admitted to this first trial, which lasted a week, and which produced only an immense number of broken teeth and jaws out of place.

It was therefore necessary to make a second appeal; and all the national and foreign newspapers were crammed with advertisements to that purpose. The king offered the post of Perpetual President of the Academy, and

the Order of the Golden Spider to whomsoever should
succeed in cracking the Crackatook nut. There was no
necessity to have a degree of Doctor of Philosophy, or
Master of Arts, to be competent to stand as a candidate.

This second trial produced five thousand candidates.
All the learned societies of Europe sent deputies to this
important assembly. Several members of the English
Royal Society were present; and a great number of critics
belonging to the leading London newspapers and literary
journals; but they were not able to stand as candidates,
because their teeth had all been broken long before in
their frequent attempts to tear to pieces the works of their
brother authors. This second trial, which lasted a fort-
night, was, alas! as fruitless as the first. The deputies of
the learned societies disputed amongst themselves, for
the honour of the association to which they respectively
belonged, as to who should break the nut; but they only
left their best teeth behind them.

As for the nut itself, its shell
did not even bear the marks
of the attempts that had
been made to crack it.

The king was in despair. He resolved, however, to strike one grand blow; and, as he had no male descendant, he declared, by means of a third article in the *Royal Gazette*, the national newspapers, and the foreign journals, that the hand of Princess Pirlipata and the inheritance of the throne should be given to him who might crack the Crackatook nut. There was one condition to this announcement; namely, that this time the candidates must be from sixteen to twenty-four years of age. The promise of such a reward excited all Germany. Competitors poured in from all parts of Europe; and they would even have come from Asia, Africa, and America, and that fifth quarter of the world which had been discovered by Christian Elias Drosselmayer and his friend the astrologer, if there had been sufficient time.

On this occasion the mechanician and the astrologer thought that the moment was now come to produce young Drosselmayer; for it was impossible for the king to offer a higher reward than that just announced. Only, certain of success as they were, and although this time

a host of princes and royal and imperial jaws had presented themselves, the mechanism and the astronomer did not appear with their young friend at the register-office until just as it was about to close; so that the name NATHANIEL DROSSELMAYER was number 11,375th, and stood last.

It was on this occasion as on the preceding ones. The 11,374 rivals of young Drosselmayer were foiled; and on the nineteenth day of the trial, at twenty-five minutes to twelve o'clock, and just as the princess accomplished her fifteenth year, the name of Nathaniel Drosselmayer was called.

The young man presented himself, accompanied by his two guardians, the mechanician and the astrologer. It was the first time that these two illustrious persons had seen the princess since they had beheld her in the cradle; and since that period great changes had taken place with her. But I must inform you, with due candour, that those changes were not to her advantage. When a child, she was shockingly ugly: she was now frightfully so.

Her form had lost, with its growth, none of its important features. It is therefore difficult to understand how those skinny legs, those flat hips, and that distorted body, could have supported such a monstrous head. And that head had the same grizzled hair—the same green eyes— the same enormous mouth—and the same cotton beard on the chin, as we have already described; only all these features were just fifteen years older.

Upon perceiving that monster of ugliness, poor Nathaniel shuddered and inquired of the mechanician and the astrologer if they were quite sure that the kernel of the Crackatook nut would restore the princess to her beauty: because, if she were to remain in that state, he was quite willing to make the trial in a matter where all the others had failed; but he should leave the honour of the marriage and the profit of the heirship of the throne to any one who might be inclined to accept them. It is hardly necessary to state that both the mechanician and

the astrologer reassured their young friend, promising that the nut, once broke, and the kernel, once eaten, Pirlipata would become that very moment the most beautiful princess on the face of the earth.

But if the sight of Princess Pirlipata had struck poor Nathaniel with dismay, I must tell you, in honour of the young man, that *his* presence had produced a very different effect upon the sensitive heart of the heiress of the crown; and she could not prevent herself from exclaiming, when she saw him, "Oh! how glad I should be if he were to break the nut!"

Thereupon the chief governess of the princess replied, "I think I have often observed to your highness, that it is not customary for a young and beautiful princess like yourself to express her opinion aloud relative to such matters."

Nathaniel was indeed calculated to turn the heads of all the princesses in the world. He wore a little military frock-coat, of a violet colour, all braided, and with golden buttons, and which his uncle had made for this solemn occasion. His breeches were of the same stuff; and his boots were so well blacked, and sat in such admirable manner, that they seemed as if they were painted. The only thing which somewhat spoilt his appearance was the ugly piece of wood fitted to the nape of his neck; but Uncle Drosselmayer had so contrived that it seemed like a little bag attached to his wig, and might at a stretch have passed as an eccentricity of the toilet, or else as a new fashion which Nathaniel's tailor was trying to push into vogue at the court.

Thus it was, that when this charming young man entered the great hall, what the princess had the

imprudence to say aloud, the other ladies present said to themselves; and there was not a person, not even excepting the king and the queen, who did not desire at the bottom of his heart that Nathaniel might prove triumphant in the adventure which he had undertaken.

On his side, young Drosselmayer approached with a confidence which encouraged the hopes that were placed in him. Having reached the steps leading to the throne, he bowed to the king and queen, then to Princess Pirlipata, and then to the spectators; after which he received the Crackatook nut from the grand master of the ceremonies, took it delicately between his fore-finger and thumb, placed it in his mouth, and gave a violent pull at the wooden balance hanging behind him.

Crack! crack!—and the shell was broken in several pieces.

He then skilfully detached the kernel from the fibres hanging to it, and presented it to the princess, bowing gracefully but respectfully at the same time; after which he closed his eyes, and began to walk backwards. At the same moment the princess swallowed the kernel; and, O! wonder! her horrible ugliness disappeared, and she became a young lady of angelic beauty. Her face seemed to have borrowed the hues of the rose and the lily: her eyes were of sparkling azure; and thick tresses, resembling masses of golden thread, flowed over her alabaster shoulders.

The trumpets and the cymbals sounded enough to make one deaf; and the shouts of the people responded to the noise of the instruments. The king, the ministers, the councillors of state, and the judges began to dance, as they had done at the birth of Pirlipata; and eau-de-cologne was obliged to be thrown in the face of the queen, who had fainted for joy.

The great tumult proved very annoying to young Nathaniel Drosselmayer, who, as you must remember, had yet to step seven paces backwards. He, however, behaved with a coolness which gave the highest hopes relative to the period when he should be called upon to reign in his turn; and he was just stretching out his leg to take the seventh step, when the queen of the mice suddenly appeared through a crevice in the floor. With horrible squeaks she ran between his legs; so that just at that very moment when the future Prince Royal placed his foot upon the ground, his heel came so fully on the body of the mouse that he stumbled in such a manner as to nearly fall.

O sorrow! At the same instant the handsome young man became as ugly as the princess was before him; his shrunken form could hardly support his enormous head; his eyes became green, haggard, and goggle; his mouth split from ear to ear; and his delicate little sprouting beard changed into a white and soft substance, which was afterward found to be cotton.

But the cause of this event was punished at the same moment that she produced it. Dame Mousey was weltering in her own blood upon the floor. Her wickedness did not therefore go without its punishment. In fact, young Drosselmayer had trampled so hard upon her with his heel, that she was crushed beyond all hope of recovery. But, while still writhing on the floor, Dame Mousey squeaked forth the following words, with all the strength of her agonizing voice:

"Crackatook! Crackatook! fatal nut that thou art,
    Through thee has Death reached me, at length, with his
        dart!
            Heigho! heigho!
But the Queen of the Mice has thousands to back her,
And my son will yet punish that wretched Nutcracker,
        I know! I know!

"Sweet life, adieu!
        Too soon snatch'd away!
And thou heaven of blue,
        And thou world so gay,
Adieu! adieu!"

The verses of Dame Mousey might have been better; but one cannot be very correct, as you will all agree, when breathing the last sigh!

And when that last sigh was rendered, a great officer of the court took up Dame Mousey by the tail, and carried her away for the purpose of interring her remains in the hole where so many of her family had been buried fifteen years and some months beforehand.

As, in the middle of all this, no one had troubled themselves about Nathaniel Drosselmayer except the mechanician and the astrologer, the princess, who was unaware of the accident which had happened, ordered the young hero to be brought into her presence; for, in spite of the lesson read to her by the governess, she was in haste to thank him. But scarcely had she perceived the unfortunate Nathaniel, than she hid her face in her hands; and, forgetting the service which he had rendered her, cried, "Turn out the horrible Nutcracker! turn him out! turn him out!"

The grand marshal of the palace accordingly took poor Nathaniel by the shoulders and pushed him down stairs. The king, who was very angry at having a Nutcracker proposed to him as his son-in-law, attacked the astrologer and the mechanician; and, instead of the income of six hundred pounds a year and the telescope of honour which he had promised the first—instead, also, of the sword set with diamonds, the Order of the Golden Spider, and the drab frock-coat, which he ought to have given the latter—he banished them both from his kingdom, granting them only twenty-four hours to cross the frontiers.

Obedience was necessary. The mechanician, the astrologer, and young Drosselmayer (now become a Nutcracker), left the capital and quitted the country. But when night came, the two learned men consulted the stars once more, and read in them that, all deformed though he were, Nathaniel would not the less become a prince and king, unless indeed he chose to remain a private individual, which was left to his own choice. This was to happen when his deformity should disappear; and that deformity would disappear when he should have commanded an army in battle—when he should have killed the seven-headed king of the mice, who was born after Dame Mousey's seven first sons had been put to death—and, lastly, when a beautiful lady should fall in love with him.

But while awaiting these brilliant destinies, Nathaniel Drosselmayer, who had left the paternal shop as the only son and heir, now returned to it in the form of a Nutcracker!

I need scarcely tell you that his father did not recognise him; and that, when Christopher Zacharias inquired of the mechanician and his friend the astrologer, what had become of his dearly-beloved son, those two illustrious persons replied, with the seriousness of learned men, that the king and the queen would not allow the saviour of the princess to leave them, and that young Nathaniel remained at court covered with honour and glory. As for the unfortunate Nutcracker, who felt how deeply painful was his situation, he uttered not a word, but resolved to await patiently the change which must some day or another take place in him. Nevertheless, I must candidly admit, that in spite of the good-nature of his disposition, he was desperately vexed with Uncle Drosselmayer, who, coming at a moment he was so little expected, and having enticed him away by so many fine promises, was the sole and only cause of the frightful misfortune that had occurred to him.

Such, my dear children, is the History of the Crackatook Nut, just as Godfather Drosselmayer told it to little Mary and Fritz; and you can now understand why people often say, when speaking of anything difficult to do, "That is a hard nut to crack."

THE UNCLE AND THE NEPHEW

If any one of my young friends now around me has ever cut himself with glass, which he has most likely done in the days of his disobedience, he must know by experience that it is a particularly disagreeable kind of cut, because it is so long in healing. Mary was, therefore, forced to stay a whole week in bed; for she always felt giddy whenever she tried to get up. But at last she got well altogether, and was able to skip about the room as she was wont to do.

You would not do my little heroine the injustice to suppose that her first visit was to any other place than the glass cupboard, which now seemed quite charming to look at. A new pane had been put in; and all the windows had been so well cleaned by Miss Trudchen, that all the trees, houses, dolls, and other toys of the Christmas eve seemed quite new, gay, and polished. But in the midst of all the treasures of her little kingdom, and before all other things, Mary perceived her Nutcracker smiling upon her from the second shelf where he was placed, and with his teeth all in as good order as ever they were. While thus joyfully examining her favourite, an idea which had more than once presented itself to the mind of Mary touched her to the quick. She was persuaded that all Godfather Drosselmayer had told her was not a mere fable, but the true history of the disagreement between the Nutcracker on one side, and the late queen of the mice and her son, the reigning king, on the other side. She, therefore, knew that the Nutcracker could be neither more nor less than Nathaniel Drosselmayer, of Nuremberg, the amiable but enchanted nephew of her godfather; for that the skilful mechanician who had figured at the court of Pirlipata's father, was Doctor Drosselmayer, she had never doubted from the moment when he introduced his drab frock-coat into his tale. This belief was strengthened when she found him losing first his hair by a sun-stroke, and then his eye by an arrow, events which had rendered necessary the invention of the ugly black patch, and of the ingenious glass wig, of which I have already spoken.

"But why did not your uncle help you, poor Nutcracker?" said Mary, as she stood at the glass cupboard, gazing up at her favourite; for she remembered that on the success of the battle depended the disenchantment of the poor little man and his elevation to the rank of king of the kingdom of toys. Then she thought that all the dolls, puppets, and little men must be well prepared to receive him as their king; for did they not obey the Nutcracker as soldiers obey a general? That indifference on the part of Godfather Drosselmayer was so much the more annoying to little Mary, because she was certain that those dolls and puppets to which, in her imagination, she gave life and motion, really did live and move.

Nevertheless, there was now no appearance of either life or motion in the cupboard, where everything was still and quiet. But Mary, rather than give up her sincere belief, thought that all this was occasioned by the sorcery of the late queen of the mice and her son; and so firm was she in this belief, that, while she gazed up at the Nutcracker, she continued to say aloud what she had only begun to say to herself.

"And yet," she resumed, "although you are unable to move, and are prevented by enchantment from saying a single word to me, I am very sure, my dear Mr. Drosselmayer, that you understand me perfectly, and that you are well aware of my good intentions with regard to you. Reckon, then, upon my support when you require it; and in the meantime, do not vex yourself. I will go straight to your uncle, and beg him to assist you; and if he only loves you a little, he is so clever that I am sure he can help you."

In spite of the eloquence of this speech, the Nutcracker did not move an inch; but it seemed to Mary that a sigh came from behind the glass, the panes of which began to sound very low, but wonderfully soft and pleasing; while it appeared to Mary that a sweet voice, like a small silver bell, said, "Dear little Mary, thou art my guardian angel! I will be thine, and Mary shall be mine!" And at these words, so mysteriously heard, Mary felt a singular sensation of happiness, in spite of the shudder which passed through her entire frame.

Twilight had now arrived; and the judge returned home, accompanied by Doctor Drosselmayer. In a few moments Miss Trudchen got tea ready, and all the family were gath-

ered round the table, talking gaily. As for Mary, she had been
to fetch her little arm-chair, and had seated herself in silence
at the feet of Godfather Drosselmayer. Taking advantage of
a moment when no one was speaking, she raised her large
blue eyes towards the doctor, and, looking earnestly at him,
said, "I now know, dear godpapa, that my Nutcracker is
your nephew, young Drosselmayer, of Nuremberg. He has
become a prince, and also a king of the kingdom of toys,
as your friend the astrologer prophesied. But you know
that he is at open war with the king of the mice. Come,
dear godpapa, tell me why you did not help him when
you were sitting astride upon the clock? and why do you
now desert him?"

And, with these words, Mary again related, amidst the
laughter of her father, her mother, and Miss Trudchen,
the events of that famous battle which she had seen. Fritz
and Godfather Drosselmayer alone did not enjoy the
whole scene.

"Where," said the godfather, "does that little girl get all
those foolish ideas which enter her head?"

"She has a very lively imagination," replied Mary's
mother; "and, after all, these are only dreams and visions
occasioned by fever."

"And I can prove *that*," shouted Fritz; "for she says that my red hussars took to flight, which cannot possibly be true—unless indeed they are abominable cowards, in which case they would not get the better of me, for I would flog them all soundly."

Then, with a singular smile, Godfather Drosselmayer took Mary upon his knees, and said with more kindness than before, "My dear child, you do not know what course you are pursuing in espousing so warmly the cause of your Nutcracker. You will have to suffer much if you persist in taking the part of one who is in disgrace; for the king of the mice, who considers him to be the murderer of his mother, will persecute him in all ways. But, in any case, remember that it is not I—but you alone—who can save him. Be firm and faithful—and all will go well."

Neither Mary nor any one else understood the words of Godfather Drosselmayer: on the contrary, those words seemed so strange to the judge, that he took the doctor's hand, felt his pulse for some moments in silence, and then said, "My dear friend, you are very feverish, and I should advise you to go home to bed."

THE DUEL

During the night, which followed the scene just related, and while the moon, shining in all its splendour, cast its bright rays through the openings in the curtains, Mary, who now slept with her mother, was awakened by a noise that seemed to come from the corner of the room, and was mingled with sharp screeches and squeakings.

"Alas!" cried Mary, who remembered to have heard the same noise on the occasion of the famous battle; "alas! the mice are coming again! Mamma, mamma, mamma!"

But her voice was stifled in her throat, in spite of all her efforts: she endeavoured to get up to run out of the room, but seemed to be nailed to her bed, unable to move her limbs. At length, turning her affrighted eyes towards the corner of the room, when the noise came, she beheld the king of the mice scraping for himself a way through the wall, and thrusting in first one of his heads, then another, then a third, and so on until the whole seven, each with a crown, made their appearance. Having entered the room, he walked several times round it like a victor who takes possession of his conquest: he then leapt with one bound upon a table that was standing near the bed. Gazing upon her with his fourteen eyes, all as bright as carbuncles, and with a gnashing of his teeth and a horrible squeaking noise, he said, "Fe, fa, fum! You must give me all your sugar-plums and your sweet cakes, little girl, and if not, I will eat up your friend the Nutcracker."

Then, having uttered this threat, he fled from the room by the same hole as he had entered by.

Mary was so frightened by this terrible apparition, that she awoke in the morning very pale and broken-hearted, the more so that she dared not mention what had taken place during the night, for fear of being laughed at. Twenty times was she on the point of telling all, either to her mother or to Fritz; but she stopped, still thinking that neither the one nor the other would believe her. It was, however, pretty clear that she must sacrifice her sugar-plums and her sweet cakes to the safety of the poor Nutcracker. She accordingly placed them all on the ledge of the cupboard that very evening.

Next morning, the judge's wife said, "I really do not know whence come all the mice that have suddenly invaded the house; but those naughty creatures have actually eaten up all my poor little Mary's sugar-plums."

The lady was not quite right; the sugar-plums and cakes were only *spoilt*, not *eaten up*; for the gluttonous king of the mice, not finding the sweet cakes as good as he expected, messed them about so that they were forced to be thrown away.

But as it was not sugar-plums that Mary liked best, she did not feel much regret at the sac-  rifice which the king of the mice had extorted from her; and, thinking that he would be content with the first con- tribution with which he had taxed her, she was much pleased at the idea of having saved Nutcracker upon such good terms.

Unfortunately her sat- isfaction was not of long duration; for the following night she was again awoke by hearing squeaking and whining close by her ears.

Alas! it was the king of the mice again, his eyes shining more horribly than on the preceding night; and, in a voice interrupted by frequent whines and squeaks, he said, "You must give me your little sugar dolls and figures made of biscuit, little girl; if not, I will eat up your friend the Nutcracker."

Thereupon the king of the mice went skipping away, and disappeared by the hole in the wall.

Next morning, Mary, now deeply afflicted, went straight to the glass cupboard, and threw a mournful look upon her figures of sugar and biscuit; and her grief was very natural, for never were such nice-looking sweet things seen before.

"Alas!" she said, as she turned towards the Nutcracker, "what would I not do for you, my dear Mr. Drosselmayer? But you must admit all the same that what I am required to do is very hard."

At these words the Nutcracker assumed so piteous an air, that Mary, who fancied that she was for ever beholding the jaws of the king of the mice opening to devour him, resolved to make this second sacrifice to save the unfortunate young man. That very evening, therefore, she placed her sugar figures and her biscuits upon the ledge of the cupboard, where the night before she had put her sugar-plums and sweet cakes. Kissing them, however, one after another, as a token of farewell, she yielded up her shepherds and shepherdesses, and her sheep, concealing behind the flock at the same time a little sugar baby with fat round cheeks, and which she loved above all the other things.

"Now really this is too bad!" cried the judge's wife next morning: "it is very clear that these odious mice have taken up their dwelling in the glass cupboard; for all poor Mary's sugar figures are eaten up."

At these words large tears started from Mary's eyes; but she dried them up almost directly, and even smiled sweetly as she thought to herself, "What matter my shepherds, shepherdesses, and sheep, since the Nutcracker is saved!"

"Mamma," cried Fritz, who was present at the time, "I must remind you that our baker has an excellent grey cat, which we might send for, and which would soon put an end to all this by snapping up the mice one after another, and even Dame Mousey herself afterwards, as well as her son the king."

"Yes," replied the judge's wife; "but that same cat would jump upon the table and shelves, and break my glasses and cups to pieces."

"Oh! there is no fear of *that*!" cried Fritz. "The baker's cat is too polite to do any such thing; and I wish I could walk along the pipes and the roofs of houses as skilfully as he can."

"No cats here, if you please!" cried the judge's wife, who could not bear those domestic animals.

"But, after all," said the judge, who overheard what was going on, "some good may follow from the remarks of Fritz: if you will not have a cat, get a mouse-trap."

"Capital!" cried Fritz: "that idea is very happy, since Godpapa Drosselmayer invented mouse-traps."

Every one now laughed; and as, after a strict search, no such thing as a mouse-trap was found in the house, the servants went to Godfather Drosselmayer, who sent back a famous one, which was baited with a bit of bacon, and placed in the spot where the mice had made such havock.

Mary went to bed with the hope that morning would find the king of the mice a prisoner in the box, to which his gluttony was almost certain to lead him. But at about eleven o'clock, and while she was in her first sleep, she was awoke by something cold and velvety that leapt about her arms and face; and, at the same moment, the whining and squeaking which she knew so well, rang in her ears. The horrible king of the mice was there—seated on her pillow, with his eyes shooting red flames and his seven mouths wide open, as if he were about to eat poor Mary up.

"I laugh at the trap—I laugh at the trap," said the king of the mice: "I shall not go into the little house, and the bacon will not tempt me. I shall not be taken: I laugh at the trap! But you must give me your picture-books and your little silk frock; if not, I will eat up your friend the Nutcracker."

You can very well understand that after such a demand as this, Mary awoke in the morning with her heart full of sorrow and her eyes full of tears. Her mother, moreover, told her nothing new when she said that the trap had remained empty, and that the king of the mice had suspected the snare. Then, as the judge's wife left the room to see after the breakfast, Mary entered her papa's room, and going up to the cupboard, said, "Alas, my dear good Mr. Drosselmayer, where will all this end? When I have given my picture-books to the king of the mice to tear, and my pretty little silk frock, which my guardian angel sent me, to rend into pieces, he will not be content, but will every day be asking me for more. And when I have nothing else

left to give him, he will perhaps eat me up in your
place. Alas! what can
a poor little girl like
me do for you, dear
good Mr. Drosselmayer?
what can I do?"

While Mary was
weeping and lament-
ing in this manner,
she observed that the
Nutcracker had a drop of blood upon his neck. From the
day when she had discovered that her favourite was the
son of the toy-man and the nephew of the Doctor, she had
left off carrying him in her arms, and had neither kissed
nor caressed him. Indeed, so great was her timidity in this
respect, that she had not even dared to touch him with
the tip of her finger. But at this moment, seeing that he
was hurt, and fearing lest his wound might be dangerous,
she took him gently out of the cupboard, and began to
wipe away with her handkerchief the drop of blood which
was upon his neck. But how great was her astonishment,
when she suddenly felt the Nutcracker moving about
in her hands! She replaced him quickly upon the shelf:
his lips quivered from ear to ear, which made his mouth
seem larger still; and, by dint of trying to speak, he con-
cluded by uttering the following words: —"Ah, dear Miss
Silberhaus—excellent friend—what do I not owe you?
and how much gratitude have I to express to you? Do not
sacrifice for me your picture-books and your silk frock;
but get me a sword—a good sword—and I will take care
of the rest!"

The Nutcracker would have said more; but his words became unintelligible—his voice sank altogether—and his eyes, for a moment animated by an expression of the softest melancholy, grew motionless and vacant. Mary felt no alarm: on the contrary, she leapt for joy, for she was very happy at the idea of being able to save the Nutcracker, without being compelled to give up her picture-books or her silk frock. One thing alone vexed her—and that was where could she find the good sword that the little man required? Mary resolved to explain her difficulty to Fritz, who, in spite of his blustering manners, she knew to be a good-natured boy. She accordingly took him up close to the glass cupboard, told him all that had happened between the Nutcracker and the king of the mice, and ended by explaining the nature of the service she required of him. The only thing which made a great impression upon Fritz was the idea that his hussars had really acted in a cowardly manner in the thickest of the battle: he therefore asked Mary if the accusations were really true; and as he knew that she never told a story, he believed her words. Then, rushing up to the cupboard, he made a speech to his soldiers, who seemed quite ashamed of themselves. But this was not all: in order to punish the whole regiment in the person of its officers, he degraded them one after the other, and expressly ordered the band not to play the *Hussar's March* during parade.

Then, turning to Mary, he said, "As for the Nutcracker, who seems to me to be a brave little fellow, I think I can manage his business; for, as I put a veteran major of horse-guards upon half pay yesterday, he having finished his time in the service, I should think he cannot want his sword any longer. It is an excellent blade, I can assure you!"

It now remained to find the major. A search was commenced, and he was found living on his half-pay in a little tavern which stood in a dark corner of the third shelf in the cupboard. As Fritz had imagined, he offered no objection to give up his sword, which had become useless to him, and which was that instant fastened to the Nutcracker's neck.

The fear which Mary now felt prevented her from sleeping all the next night; and she was so wide awake that she heard the clock strike twelve in the room where the cupboard was. Scarcely had the hum of the last stroke ceased, when strange noises came from the direction of the cupboard; and then there was a great clashing of swords, as if two enemies were fighting in mortal combat. Suddenly one of the duellists gave a squeak!

"The king of the mice!" cried Mary, full of joy and terror at the same time.

There was then a dead silence; but presently some one knocked gently—very gently—at the door; and a pretty little voice said, "Dearest Miss Silberhaus, I have glorious news for you: open the door, I beseech you!"

Mary recognized the voice of young Drosselmayer. She hastily put on her little frock, and opened the door. The Nutcracker was there, holding the blood-stained sword in his right hand and a candle in his left. The moment he saw Mary he knelt down, and said, "It is you alone, O dearest lady! who have nerved me up with the chivalrous courage which I have just shown, and who gave me strength

to fight that insolent wretch who dared to threaten you. The vile king of the mice is bathed in his blood. Will you, O lady! deign to accept the trophies of the victory—trophies that are offered by the hand of a knight who is devoted to you until death?"

With these words the Nutcracker drew from his left arm the seven gold crowns of the king of the mice, which he had placed there as if they were bracelets, and which he now offered to Mary, who received them with joy.

The Nutcracker, encouraged by this amiability on her part, then rose and spoke thus: —"Oh! dear Miss Silberhaus, now that I have conquered my enemy, what beautiful things can I show you, if you would have the condescension to go with me only a few paces hence! Oh! do not refuse me—do not refuse me, dear lady—I implore you!"

Mary did not hesitate a moment to follow the Nutcracker, knowing how great were her claims upon his gratitude, and being quite certain that he had no evil intention towards her.

"I will follow you," she said, "my dear Mr. Drosselmayer; but you must not take me very far, nor keep me long away, because I have not yet slept a wink."

"I will choose the shortest, although the most difficult, path," said the Nutcracker; and, thus speaking, he led the way, Mary following him.

THE KINGDOM OF TOYS

They both reached, in a short time, a large old cupboard standing in a passage near the door, and which was used as a clothes'-press. There the Nutcracker stopped; and Mary observed, to her great astonishment, that the folding-doors of the cupboard, which were nearly always kept shut, were now wide open, so that she could see plainly her father's travelling-cloak lined with fox-skin, which was hanging over the other clothes. The Nutcracker climbed very skilfully along the border of the cloak; and, clinging to the braiding, he reached the large cape, which, fastened by a piece of lace, fell over the back of the cloak. From beneath this cape the Nutcracker drew down a pretty little ladder of cedar-wood, which he placed in such a manner that the foot touched the bottom of the cupboard, and the top was lost in the sleeve of the cloak.

"Now, dear young lady," said the Nutcracker, "have the goodness to give me your hand and ascend with me."

Mary complied; and scarcely had she glanced up the sleeve, when a brilliant light burst upon her view, and she suddenly found herself transported into the midst of a fragrant meadow,  which glittered as if it were strewed with precious stones.

"Oh! how charming!" cried Mary, dazzled by the sight, "where are we?"

"We are in the Field of Sugar-candy, Miss; but we will not remain here, unless you wish to do so. Let us pass through this door."

Then Mary observed a beautiful gate through which they left the field. The gate seemed to be made of white marble, red marble, and blue marble; but when Mary drew near it she saw that it was made of preserves, candied orange-peel, burnt almonds, and sugared raisins. This was the reason, as she learnt from the Nutcracker, why that gate was called the Gate of Burnt Almonds.

The gate opened into a long gallery, the roof of which was supported by pillars of barley-sugar. In the gallery there were five monkeys, all dressed in red, and playing music, which, if it were not the most melodious in the world, was at least the most original. Mary made so much haste to see more, that she did not even perceive that she was walking upon a pavement of pistachio-nuts and macaroons, which she took for marble. At length she reached the end of the gallery, and scarcely was she in the open air, when she found herself surrounded by the most delicious perfumes, which came from a charming little

forest that opened before her. This forest, which would have been dark were it not for the quantity of lamps that it contained, was lighted up in so brilliant a manner that it was easy to distinguish the golden and silver fruits, which were suspended to branches ornamented with white ribands and nosegays, resembling marriage favours.

"Oh! my dear Mr. Drosselmayer," cried Mary, "what is the name of this charming place, I beseech you?"

"We are now in the Forest of Christmas, Miss," answered the Nutcracker; "and it is here that people come to fetch the trees to which the presents sent by the guardian angels are fastened."

"Oh!" continued Mary, "may I not remain here one moment? Everything is so nice here and smells so sweet!"

The Nutcracker clapped his hands together; and several shepherds and shepherdesses, hunters and huntresses, came out of the forest, all so delicate and white that they seemed made of refined sugar. They carried on their shoulders an arm-chair, made of chocolate, incrusted with angelica, in which they placed a cushion of jujube, inviting Mary most politely to sit down. Scarcely had she done so when, as at operas, the shepherds and shepherdesses, the hunters and huntresses, took their places and began to dance a charming ballet to an accompaniment of horns and bugles, which the hunters blew with such good will that their faces became flushed just as if they were made of conserve of roses. Then, the dance being finished, they all disappeared in a grove.

"Pardon me, dear Miss Silberhaus," said the Nutcracker, holding out his hand towards Mary—"pardon me for having exhibited to you so poor a ballet; but those simpletons can do nothing better than repeat, over and over again, the same step. As for the hunters, they blew their bugles

as if they were afraid of them; and I can promise you that
I shall not let it pass so quietly. But let us leave those creatures for the present, and continue our walk, if you please."

"I really found it all very delightful," said Mary, accept-
ing the invitation of the Nutcracker; "and it seems to me,
my dear Mr. Drosselmayer, that you are harsh towards the
little dancers."

The Nutcracker made a face, as much as to say, "We
shall see; but your plea in their favour shall be considered." They then continued their journey, and reached a
river which seemed to send forth all the sweet scents that
perfumed the air.

"This," said the Nutcracker, without even waiting to
be questioned by Mary, "is the River of Orange Juice. It
is one of the smallest in the kingdom; for, save in respect
to its sweet odour, it cannot be compared to the River of
Lemonade, which falls into the southern sea, or the Sea of
Punch. The Lake of Sweet Whey is also finer: it joins the
northern sea, which is called the Sea of Milk of Almonds."

At a short distance was a little village, in which the
houses, the church, and the parsonage were all brown; the
roofs however were gilt, and the walls were resplendent
with incrustations of red, blue, and white sugar-plums.

"This is the Village of Sweet Cake," said the Nutcracker; "it is a pretty little place, as you perceive, and is situate on the Streamlet of Honey. The inhabitants are very agreeable to look upon; but they are always in a bad humour, because they are constantly troubled with the tooth-ache. But, my dear Miss Silberhaus," continued the Nutcracker, "do not let us stop at all the villages and little towns of the kingdom. To the capital! to the capital!"

The Nutcracker advanced, still holding Mary's hand, but walking more confidently than he hitherto had done; for Mary, who was full of curiosity, kept by his side, light as a bird. At length, after the expiration of some minutes, the odour of roses was spread through the air, and everything around them now seemed to be of a rose-tint. Mary remarked that this was the perfume and the reflection of a River of Essence of Roses, which flowed along, its waves rippling melodiously. Upon the sweet-scented waters, silver swans, with collars of gold round their necks, swam gently along, warbling the most delicate songs, so that this harmony, with which they were apparently much pleased, made the diamond fishes leap up around them.

"Ah!" cried Mary, "this is the pretty river which Godpapa Drosselmayer made me at Christmas; and I am the girl who played with the swans!"

THE JOURNEY

The Nutcracker tapped his hands together once more; and, at the moment, the River of Essence of Roses began to rise visibly; and from its swelling waves came forth a chariot made of shells, and covered with precious stones that glittered in the sun. It was drawn by golden dolphins; and four charming little Moors, with caps made of scales of gold-fish and clothes of humming-birds' feathers, leapt upon the bank. They first carried Mary, and then the Nutcracker, very gently down to the chariot, which instantly began to advance upon the stream.

You must confess that it was a ravishing spectacle, and one which might even be compared to the voyage of Cleopatra upon the Cydnus, which you read of in Roman History, to behold little Mary in the chariot of shells, surrounded by perfume, and floating on the waves of essence of roses. The golden dolphins that drew the chariot, tossed up their heads, and threw into the air the glittering jets of rosy crystal, which fell in variegated showers of all the colours of the rainbow. Moreover, that pleasure might penetrate every sense, a soft music began to echo round; and sweet silvery voices were heard singing in the following manner:

> "Who art thou, thus floating where essence of rose
> In a stream of sweet perfume deliciously flows?
>   Art thou the Fairies' Queen?
> Say, dear little fishes that gleam in the tide;
> Or answer, ye cygnets that gracefully glide
>   Upon that flood serene!"

And all this time the little Moors, who stood behind the seat on the chariot of shells, shook two parasols, hung with bells, in such a manner that those sounds formed an accompaniment to the vocal melody. And Mary, beneath the shade of the parasols, leant over the waters, each wave of which as it passed reflected her smiling countenance.

In this manner she traversed the River of Essence of Roses and reached the bank on the opposite side. Then,

when they were within an oar's length of the shore, the little Moors leapt, some into the water, others on the bank, the whole forming a chain so as to convey Mary and the Nutcracker ashore upon a carpet made of angelica, all covered with mint-drops.

The Nutcracker now conducted Mary through a little grove, which was perhaps prettier than the Christmas Forest, so brilliantly did each tree shine, and so sweetly did they all smell with their own peculiar essence. But what was most remarkable was the quantity of fruits hanging to the branches, those fruits being not only of singular colour and transparency—some yellow as the topaz, others red like the ruby—but also of a wondrous perfume.

"We are now in the Wood of Preserved Fruits," said the Nutcracker, "and beyond that boundary is the capital."

And, as Mary thrust aside the last branches, she was stupefied at beholding the extent, the magnificence, and the novel appearance of the city which rose before her upon a mound of flowers. Not only did the walls and steeples glitter with the most splendid colours, but, in respect to the shape of the buildings, it was impossible to see any so beautiful upon the earth. The fortifications and the gates were built of candied fruits, which shone in the sun with their

own gay colours, all rendered more brilliant still by the crystallised sugar that covered them. At the principal gate, which was the one by which they entered, silver soldiers presented arms to them, and a little man, clad in a dressing-gown of gold brocade, threw himself into the Nutcracker's arms, crying "Oh! dear prince, have you come at length? Welcome—welcome to the City of Candied Fruits!"

Mary was somewhat astonished at the great title given to the Nutcracker; but she was soon drawn from her surprise by the noise of an immense quantity of voices all chattering at the same time; so that she asked the Nutcracker if there were some disturbance or some festival in the Kingdom of Toys?

"There is nothing of all that, dear Miss Silberhaus," answered the Nutcracker; "but the City of Candied Fruits is so happy a place, and all its people are so joyful, that they are constantly talking and laughing. And this is always the same as you see it now. But come with me; let us proceed, I implore of you."

Mary, urged by her own curiosity and by the polite invitation of the Nutcracker, hastened her steps, and soon found herself in a large market-place, which had seen the most magnificent aspects that could possibly be seen. All the houses around were of sugar, open with fretwork, and having balcony over balcony; and in the middle of the market-place was an enormous cake, from the inside of which flowed four fountains, namely, lemonade, orangeade, sweet milk, and gooseberry syrup. The basins around were filled with whipped syllabub, so delicious in appearance, that several well-dressed persons publicly ate of it by means of spoons. But the most agreeable and amusing part of the whole scene, was the crowd of little people who walked about, arm-in-arm, by the thousands and tens of thousands, all laughing, singing, and chattering at the tops of their voices, so that Mary could now account for the joyous din which she had heard. Besides the inhabitants of the capital, there were men of all countries—Armenians, Jews, Greeks, Tyrolese, officers, soldiers, clergymen, monks, shepherds, punches, and all kinds of funny people, such as one meets with in the world.

Presently the tumult redoubled at the entrance of a street looking upon the great square; and the people stood aside to allow the cavalcade to pass. It was the Great Mogul, who was carried upon a palanquin, attended by ninety-three lords of his kingdom and seven hundred slaves: but, at the same time, it happened that from the opposite street the Grand Sultan appeared on horseback, followed by three hundred janissaries. The two sovereigns had always been rivals, and therefore enemies; and this feeling made it impossible for their attendants to meet each other without quarrelling. It was even much worse, as you may well suppose, when those two powerful monarchs found themselves face to face: in the first place there was a great confusion, from the midst of which the citizens sought to save them-

selves; but cries of fury and despair were soon heard, for a gardener, in the act of running away, had knocked off the head of a Brahmin, greatly respected by his own class; and the Grand Sultan's horse had knocked down a frightened punch, who endeavoured to creep between the animal's legs to get away from the riot. The din was increasing, when the gentleman in the gold brocade dressing-gown, who had saluted the Nutcracker by the title of "Prince" at the gate of the city, leapt to the top of the huge cake with a single bound; and having run a silvery sweet-toned bell three times, cried out three times, "Confectioner! confectioner! confectioner!"

That instant did the tumult subside and the combatants separate. The Grand Sultan was brushed, for he was covered with dust; the Brahmin's head was fixed on, with the injunction that he must not sneeze for three days, for fear it should fall off again; and order was restored. The pleasant sports began again, and every one hastened to quench his thirst with the lemonade, the orangeade, the sweet milk, or the gooseberry syrup, and to regale himself with the whip-syllabub.

"My dear Mr. Drosselmayer," said Mary, "what is the cause of the influence exercised upon those little folks by the word *confectioner* repeated thrice?"

"I must tell you, Miss," said the Nutcracker, "that the people of the City of Candied Fruits believe, by experience, in the transmigration of souls, and are in the power of a superior principle, called *confectioner*, which principle can bestow on each individual what form he likes by merely baking, for a shorter or longer period, as the case may be. Now, as everyone believes his own existing shape to be the best, he does not like to change it. Hence the magic influence of the word confectioner upon the head of the City of Candied Fruits, when pronounced by the chief magistrate. It is sufficient, as you perceive, to appease all that tumult; everyone in an instant, forgets earthly things, broken ribs, and bumps upon the head; and, restored to himself, says, '*What is man? and what may he not become?*'"

While they were thus talking, they reached the entrance of the palace, which shed around a rosy lustre, and was surmounted by a hundred light and elegant towers. The walls were strewed with nosegays, of violets, narcissi, tulips, and jasmine, which set off with their various hues the rose-coloured ground from which they stood forth. The great dome in the centre was covered with thousands of gold and silver stars.

"O, heavens!" exclaimed Mary, "what is that wonderful building?"

"The Palace of Sweet Cake," answered the Nutcracker; "and it is one of the most famous monuments in the capital of the Kingdom of Toys."

Nevertheless, lost in wonder as she was, Mary could not help observing that the roof of one of the great towers was totally wanting and that the little gingerbread men, mounted on a scaffold of cinnamon, were occupied in repairing it. She was about to question the Nutcracker relative to this accident, when he said, "Alas! It is only a disgrace, if not with absolute ruin. The giant Glutton ate up the top of that tower; and he was already on the point of biting the dome, when the people hastened to give him as a tribute the quarter of the city called Almond and Honey-cake District, together with a large portion of the Forest of Angelica, in consideration of which he agreed to take himself off without making any worse ravages than those which you see."

At that moment a soft and delicious music was heard. The gates of the palace opened themselves, and twelve little pages came forth, carrying in their hands branches of aromatic herbs, lighted like torches. Their heads were made of pearl, six of them had bodies made of rubies, and the six others of emeralds, wherewith they trotted joyously along upon two little feet of gold, sculptured with all the taste and care of Benvenuto Cellini.

They were followed by four ladies, about the same size as Miss Clara, Mary's new doll; but all so splendidly dressed and so richly adorned, that Mary was not at a loss to perceive in them the royal princesses of the City of Preserved Fruits. They all four, upon perceiving the Nutcracker, hastened to embrace him with the utmost tenderness, exclaiming at the same time, and as it were with one voice, "Oh! Prince—dear prince! Dear—dear brother!"

The Nutcracker seemed much moved; he wiped away the tears which flowed from his eyes, and, taking Mary by the hand, said, in a feeling tone, to the four princesses, "My dear sisters, this is Miss Silberhaus whom I now introduce to you. She is the daughter of Chief-Justice Silberhaus, of Nuremberg, a gentleman of the highest respectability. It is this young lady who saved my life; for, if at the moment when I lost a battle she had not thrown her shoe at the king of the mice—and, again, if she had not afterward lent me the sword of a major whom her brother had placed on the half-pay list—I should even now be sleeping in my tomb, or what is worse, be devoured by the king of the mice. "Ah! My dear Miss Silberhaus," cried the Nutcracker, with an enthusiasm which he could not controul, "Pirlipata, although the daughter of a king, was not worthy to unloose the latchet of your pretty little shoes."

"Oh! No—no; certainly not!" repeated the four princesses in chorus; and, throwing their arms round Mary's neck, they cried, "Oh! Noble liberatrix of our dear and much-loved prince and brother! Oh! Excellent Miss Silberhaus!"

And, with these exclamations, which their heart-felt joy cut short, the four princesses conducted the Nutcracker and Mary into the palace, made them sit down upon beautiful little sofas of cedar-wood, covered with golden flowers, and then insisted upon preparing a banquet with their own hands. With this object, they hastened to fetch a number of little vases and bowls made of the finest Japanese porcelain, and silver knives, forks, spoons, and other articles of the table. They then brought in the finest fruits and most delicious sugar-plums that Mary had ever seen, and began to bustle about so nimbly that Mary was at no loss to perceive how well they understood everything connected with cooking. Now, as Mary herself was well acquainted with such matters, she wished inwardly to take a share in all that was going on; and, as if she understood Mary's wishes, the most beautiful of the Nutcracker's four sisters, handed her a little golden mortar, saying, "Dear liberatrix of my brother, pound me some sugar-candy, if you please."

Mary hastened to do as she was asked; and while she was pounding the sugar-candy in the mortar, when a delicious music came forth, the Nutcracker began to relate all his adventures: but, strange as it was, it seemed to Mary during that recital, as if the words of young Drosselmayer and the noise of the pestle came gradually more and more indistinct to her ears. In a short time she seemed to be surrounded by a light vapour turned into a silvery mist, which spread more and more densely around her, so that it presently concealed the Nutcracker and the princesses from her sight. Strange songs, which reminded her of those she had heard on the River of Essence of Roses, met her ears, commingled with the increasing murmur of waters; and then Mary thought that the waves flowed beneath her, raising her up in their swell. She felt as if she were rising high up—higher—and higher; when, suddenly, down she fell from a precipice that she could not measure.

Conclusion

One does not fall several thousand feet without awaking. Thus it was that Mary awoke; and, on awaking, she found herself in her little bed. It was broad daylight, and her mother, who was standing by her, said, "Is it possible to be so lazy as you are? Come, get up, and dress yourself, dear little Mary, for breakfast is waiting."

"Oh! my dear mamma," said Mary, opening her eyes wide with astonishment, "whither did young Mr. Drosselmayer

take me last night? And what splendid things did he show me?"

Then Mary related all that I have just told you; and when she had done her mother said, "You have had a very long and charming dream, dear little Mary; but now that you are awake, you must forget it all, and come and have your breakfast."

But Mary, while she dressed herself, persisted in maintaining that she had really seen all she spoke of. Her mother accordingly went to the cupboard and took out the Nutcracker, who, according to custom, was upon the third shelf. Bringing it to her daughter, she said, "How can you suppose, silly child, that this puppet, which is made of wood and cloth, can be alive, or move, or think?"

But, my dear mamma," said Mary, perpetually, I am well aware that the Nutcracker is none other than young Mr. Drosselmayer, the nephew of godpapa."

At that moment Mary heard a loud shout of laughter behind her.

It was the judge, Fritz, and Miss Trudchen, who made themselves merry at her expense.

"Ah!" cried Mary, "how can you laugh at me, dear papa, and at my poor Nutcracker? He spoke very respectfully of you, nevertheless, when we went to the Palace of Sweet Cake, and he introduced me to his sisters."

The shouts of laughter redoubled to such an extent that Mary began to see the necessity of giving some proof of the truth of what she said, for fear of being treated as a simpleton. She therefore went into the adjoining room and brought back a little box in which she had carefully placed the seven crowns of the king of the mice.

"Here, mamma," she said, "are the seven crowns of the king of the mice, which the Nutcracker gave me last night as a proof of his victory."

The judge's wife, full of surprise, took the seven little crowns, which were made of an unknown but very brilliant metal, and were carved with a delicacy of which human hands were incapable. The judge himself could not take his eyes off them, and considered them to be so precious, that, in spite of the prayers of Fritz, he would not let him touch one of them.

The judge and his wife then pressed Mary to tell them whence came those little crowns; but she could only persist in what she had said already: and when her father, annoyed at what he heard and at what he considered obstinacy on her part, called her a little "story-teller," she burst into tears, exclaiming, "Alas! unfortunate child that I am! What would you have me tell you?"

At that moment the door opened, and the doctor made his appearance.

"What is the matter?" he said, "and what have they done to my little god-daughter that she cries and sobs like this? What is it? what is it all?"

The judge acquainted Doctor Drosselmayer with all that had occurred; and, when the story was ended, he showed him the seven crowns. But scarcely had the doctor seen them, when he burst out laughing, and said, "Well, really this is too good! These are the seven crowns that

I used to wear to my watch-chain some years ago, and which I gave to my god-daughter on the occasion of her second birthday. Do you not remember, my dear friend?"

But the judge and his wife could not recollect anything about the present stated to have been given. Nevertheless, believing what the godfather said, their countenances became more calm. Mary, upon seeing this, ran up to Doctor Drosselmayer, saying, "But you know all, god-papa! confess that the Nutcracker is your nephew, and that it was he who gave me the seven crowns."

But Godfather Drosselmayer did not at all seem to like these words; and his face became so gloomy, that the judge called little Mary to him, and taking her upon his knees, said "Listen to me, my dear child, for I wish to speak to you very seriously. Do me the pleasure, once for all, to put an end to these silly ideas; because, if you should again assert that this ugly and deformed Nutcracker is the nephew of our friend the doctor, I give you due warning that I will throw, not only the Nutcracker, but all the other toys, Miss Clara amongst them, out of the window."

Poor Mary was therefore unable to speak any more of all the fine things with which her imagination was filled but you can well understand that when a person has once travelled in such a fine place as the Kingdom of Toys, and seen such a delicious town as the City of Preserved Fruits, were it only for an hour, it is not easy to forget such sights.

Mary therefore endeavoured to speak of her brother of the whole business; but she had lost all of his confidence since the moment when she had said that his hussars had taken to flight. Convinced, therefore, that Mary was a story-teller, as her father had said so, he restored his officers to the rank from which he had reduced them, and allowed the band to play as usual the *Hussar's March*—a step which did not prevent Mary from entertaining her own opinion relative to their courage.

Many dared not therefore speak further of her adventures. Nevertheless, the remembrance of the Kingdom of Toys followed her without ceasing; and when she thought of all that, she looked upon it as it were still in the Christmas Forest, or on the River of Essence of Roses, or in the City of Preserved Fruits;—so that, instead of playing with her toys as she had been wont to do, she remained

silent and pensive, occupied only with her own thoughts, while every one called her "the little dreamer."

But one day, when the doctor, with his wig laid upon the ground, his tongue thrust into one corner of his mouth, and the sleeves of his yellow coat turned up, was mending a clock by the aid of a long pointed instrument, it happened that Mary, who was seated near the glass cupboard contemplating the Nutcracker, and buried in her own thoughts, suddenly said, quite forgetful that both the doctor and her mamma were close by, "Ah! my dear Mr. Drosselmayer, if you were not a little man made of wood, as my papa declares, and if you really were alive, I would not do as Princess Pirlipata did, and desert you because, in serving me, you had ceased to be a handsome young man; for I love you sincerely!"

But scarcely had she uttered these words, when there was such a noise in the room, that Mary fell off her chair in a fainting fit.

When she came to herself, she found that she was in the arms of her mother, who said, "How is it possible that a great girl like you, I ask, can be so foolish as to fall off your chair—and just at the moment, too, when young Mr. Drosselmayer, who has finished his travels, arrives at Nuremberg? Come, wipe your eyes, and be a good girl."

Indeed, as Mary wiped her eyes, the door opened and Godpapa Drosselmayer, with his glass wig upon his head, his hat under his arm, and his drab frock-coat upon his back, entered the room. He wore a smiling countenance, and held by the hand a young man, who, although very little, was handsome. This young man wore a superb frock-coat of red velvet embroidered with gold, white silk stockings, and shoes brilliantly polished. He had a charming nose-

gay on the bosom of his shirt, and was very dandified with his curls and hair-powder; moreover, long tresses, neatly braided, hung behind his back. The little sword that he wore by his side was brilliant with precious stones; and the hat which he carried under his arm was of the finest silk.

The amiable manners of this young man showed who he was directly; for scarcely had he entered the room, when he placed at Mary's feet a quantity of magnificent toys and nice confectionary—chiefly sweet cake and sugar-plum, the finest she had ever tasted, save in the Kingdom of Toys. As for Fritz, the doctor's nephew seemed to have guessed his martial taste, for he brought him a sword with a blade of the finest Damascus steel. At table, when the dessert was placed upon it, the amiable youth cracked nuts for all the company: the hardest could not resist his teeth for a moment. He placed them in his mouth with his right hand; with the left he pulled his hair behind; and, crack! the shell was broken.

Mary had become very red when she first saw that pretty little gentleman; but she blushed deeper still, when,

after the dessert, he invited her to go with him into the room where the glass cupboard was.

"Yes, go my dear children, and amuse yourselves together," said Godpapa Drosselmayer: "I do not want that room any more to-day, since all the clocks of my friend the judge now go well."

The two young people proceeded to the room; but scarcely was young Drosselmayer alone with Mary, when he fell upon one knee, and spoke thus:

"My dear Miss Silberhaus, you see at your feet the happy Nathaniel Drosselmayer, whose life you saved on this very spot. You also said that you would not have repulsed me, as Princess Pirlipata did, if, in serving *you*, I had become hideous. Now, as the spell which the queen of the mice threw upon me was destined to lose all its power on that day when, in spite of my ugly face, I should be beloved by a young and beautiful girl, I at that moment ceased to be a vile Nutcracker and resumed my proper shape, which is not disagreeable, as you may see. Therefore, my dear young lady, if you still possess the same sentiments in respect to myself, do me the favour to bestow your much-loved hand upon me, share my throne and my crown, and reign with me over the Kingdom of Toys, of which I ere now become the king."

Then Mary raised young Drosselmayer gently, and said, "You are an amiable and a good king, sir; and as you have moreover a charming kingdom, adorned with magnificent palaces, and possessing a very happy people, I receive you as my future husband, provided my parents give their consent."

Thereupon, as the door of the room had opened very gently without the two young folks having heard it, so occupied were they with their own sentiments, the judge, his wife, and Godpapa Drosselmayer came forward, crying "Bravo!" with all their might; which made Mary as red as a cherry. But the young man was not abashed; and, advancing towards the judge and his wife, he bowed gracefully to them, paid them a handsome compliment, and ended by soliciting the hand of Mary in marriage. The request was immediately granted.

That same day Mary was engaged to Nathaniel Drosselmayer, on condition that the marriage should not take place for a year.

At the expiration of the year, the bridegroom came to fetch the bride in a little carriage of mother of pearl incrusted with gold and silver, and drawn by ponies of the size of sheep, but which were of countless worth, because there were none like them in the world. The young king took his bride to the Palace of Sweet Cake, where they were married by the chaplain. Twenty-two thousand little people, all covered with pearls, diamonds, and brilliant stones, danced at the bridal.

Even at the present day, Mary is still queen of that beautiful country, where may be seen brilliant forests of Christmas; rivers of orangeade, sweet milk, and essence of roses; transparent palaces of sugar whiter than snow and cleaner than ice;—in a word, all kinds of wonderful and extraordinary things may there be seen by those who have eyes sharp enough to discover them.